*The Years of the Beast*

# THE YEARS OF THE BEAST

*A Novel of the Last Days*

by

Leon Chambers

Beacon Hill Press of Kansas City
Kansas City, Missouri

Copyright, 1979
Beacon Hill Press of Kansas City

ISBN: 0-8341-0574-8

Printed in the
United States of America

# Contents

# Introduction

This is the story of Dr. Judas Goldbar and his rise from a college campus to become the ruler of the world. In all of history, his rise is without equal and is beyond human explanation. Goldbar won the confidence of the West German people and, as their Prime Minister, armed them until they held an overwhelming military superiority over the rest of the world.

In quick succession, he united West and East Germany, formed an alliance with the Common Market Nations of Europe, became the Prime Minister of the United Nations of Europe, then leader of the Alliance of the World. Ultimately he ruled as the Prince of This World.

At first he moved like a kindly shepherd gathering the troubled people of the world together under his protective care. Once he had dominated them, he turned in fierce hatred upon those whom he had conquered.

Goldbar was assassinated but was resurrected by satanic power. From the time of his resurrection, he was aware of the supernatural power that lived in him. He yielded himself to Satan and became the Beast that ruled the world. Some called him Antichrist.

This story also recounts the experiences of a group of Tribulation Christians in the United States who, though persecuted and suffering, managed to live through the seven years of the Tribulation under the Beast.

# 1

# Foolish Virgins

*Afterward came also the other virgins, saying, Lord,*
*Lord, open to us. But he answered and said, Verily I say*
*unto you, I know you not* (Matt. 25:11-12).

### An Explanation

This manuscript containing information on the Tribulation was sent to me as director of the Office of Vital
Documents, Jerusalem, Year 1 of the Kingdom of Jesus
Christ. The scholars have agreed that it is authentic and at
the same time the most vivid description of the years of the
Tribulation that we have been able to find for the government archives. It is my opinion that the world should know
this story. Dr. Judas Goldbar, who called himself "Prince
of This World" and who was called the "Beast" by the
Tribulation Christians, is dead. His government has fallen
to the armies of the Kingdom of Jesus Christ; so there is no
harm that can come to anyone from this publication.

Investigation has authenticated that the author is
Stephen Miles. Preceding the Tribulation, he was an
obscure teacher in a small church college in the United

States of America. He knew the promises of the coming of Christ to rapture away His Church, but he refused to take them seriously until the Rapture was a reality. He became a Christian during the Tribulation. His story, however, can best be told in his own words.

## The Years of the Beast

I sit here in an almost stuporous state of waiting— waiting blended with dread and, above all, fear. It must be the feeling of a man on death row expecting execution but with no idea of how or when he will die. I am possessed by a black and nameless fear. I know that the world is entering the Tribulation described in the Revelation. I also know that Satan will be the power behind a world government ruled by a man called the Beast, or Antichrist. He will imitate Hitler's persecutions but, by comparison, Hitler's onslaught on the Jews will be tame. This ruler will try to exterminate both Jews and Tribulation Christians. In doing so, half of the world's population will be killed. How Satan will do this, I don't know. So I must wait.

I missed the Rapture of the Church, but that cannot be laid to ignorance. Memories of past opportunities haunt me, and realization of rejected truth tortures me. The dullness of fatalism poisons each muscle and drains my body of energy. I would like just to sit here in hiding, withdrawing farther into the shadows until I could vanish in the darkness and escape my very existence. But this is not a mere bad dream. Reality drags me back with a biting conscience and a somber mind.

From my hiding place in an abandoned coal mine near the small town where I was born, I intend to observe and record the closing drama of man on this earth.

For me, the beginning of the end came on the night of December 24. I left my apartment near Church College to spend Christmas Day with my parents. I turned on the car radio to keep me company for the drive home. There was nothing really different about the news; it was all about Dr. Judas Goldbar, Prime Minister of Germany: "Dr. Goldbar brings peace to Europe" and "Dr. Goldbar brings peace to the world." I remember thinking how quickly the prime minister had become the major figure on the world scene. But I paid little attention to the radio. I was in no mood to hear more of Goldbar.

The trip was passing without special event. Nothing audible or visible happened to prepare me for the events ahead.

It was midnight when I entered the one large city between Church College and home. The traffic was unusually heavy for the late hour, but that could be expected on Christmas Eve.

Mystery reigned from that point on. Suddenly the traffic went wild. Cars crashed into buildings, crossed center lanes to slam into oncoming traffic. People flooded into the streets screaming—some running out into the traffic as if they had gone berserk. With the wide use of narcotics and liquor, I concluded that all this bizarre behavior was the result of drunken Christmas parties.

I quickly turned off the radio so that I could concentrate on my driving. I recall glancing at my watch. It was one minute past midnight. That made it Christmas Day.

To avoid what I reasoned to be drunk and unruly people, I turned onto a side street, only to find peril in the air. A plane was coming in dangerously low over the city. Was the pilot asleep? Drunk? Ill? There was no way now for him to avoid a crash. I heard a sound like the explosion of a bomb and saw a hotel erupt into an inferno.

I arrived at the edge of the city with a deep sigh of

11

relief. When I looked back to bid the city farewell, I was surprised to see at least a half dozen fires.

For the first time, I experienced an uneasy feeling as if some strange power were hovering in the darkness. As I drove, I continued to ponder this strange, sinister-laden night. The conviction that unearthly events were taking place grew stronger as I left the suburbs for the open highway. I was not frightened by these events, but I did feel uneasy—a strange feeling of foreboding.

With the city behind me, things began to improve. The moon showered its light upon the earth so brightly that I could have easily driven without the headlights. Trees, buildings, and the entire landscape refused to fade together; each boldly claimed its own identity in the brightness of the moon. It was the beauty of the moon that rescued me from the somber and strange feeling that something evil lurked in the night.

Now, however, it was because of the brightness of the moonlight that I was forced back into my feeling of uneasiness. As I passed a familiar rural cemetery, I noticed that several of the graves had been opened. Even at a distance I could easily see the individual tombstones that had fallen over. Clods of earth appeared to have been thrown outward as if the graves had been opened in a hurry from within.

I reflected, "This is one night in which a lot of people have gone raving mad. How else can one account for cars off the road, planes crashing into hotels, people running into the traffic, and graves being opened?"

I was still trying to grapple logically with these facts when I drove into the county seat near my home. It was 1:15 on the courthouse clock. The downtown area was empty, but lights were on in most of the houses.

As I left the little town, I was again heartened by the bright moon that glowed on the trees, ridges, and farms. I

12

no longer felt despondent or dejected. A feeling of serenity, intangible but real, came over me. I felt surrounded by softness, brightness, a tranquility that seemed to penetrate to the depths of my being. I am sure that for this moment I felt the exultation that some Christians call "being blessed."

I kept looking at the moon. I had never known it to be so radiant. It was as if the heavens knew a secret that they could not share with me. I recalled the star that led the wise men to Christ on the first Christmas. Was the moon chosen tonight to tell the world of another visit by Christ? I dismissed the thought with a shrug of my shoulders.

For the moment I forgot the moon, because in quick succession I passed two more cemeteries that were also in the process of being moved. At least a fourth of the graves were open. The logical conclusion was that a new road was to be built which required the relocating of the cemeteries. There was mystery, however. Why were the open graves scattered throughout the cemeteries? If the highway department were moving the graves, they would have opened them systematically, not in a random way.

But soon the wonder of the night again erased my concern for strange happenings. There was a lonely loveliness, a satin softness in the nearness of the moon that comforted me.

Although intoxicated by the beauty of the night, I did not overlook the left turn onto a rural road that soon brought me to the small town of my birth. The buildings were robed in shadows but easily visible on this unusually bright night. There was something about being back home that made me feel at peace with myself and the world.

I drove across the railroad. A sharp right and I would be at my father's farm on the edge of the small town. Now I was in the shadow of the giant oaks that circled the front of the house. The trees stood tall and ageless. The house, as I expected, was dark. No Christmas party here. My parents had been sleeping for hours. Just a few knocks would bring Dad to the door.

Before I got out of the car Jack, the family dog, met me. Opening the car door, I stepped out into the yard where he joined me. Stroking him, I stood reminiscing. The stimulation of the night's drive made my memory keen and accurate. I could see the family as they had gathered on each Fourth of July. I heard again the laughter of the children and saw again the contented faces of the adults as they talked about the farms and the August revival. Though alone, I was not alone. Never had I been so conscious of unseen spirits moving around me. It seemed that the eternal ages watched, whispered, and waited. Waited for what? The memories brought a tide of loneliness for my childhood. Memory of the homeplace was sacred because of my love for those who had lived here.

Vivid scenes from the past flooded in. I remembered well the summer revivals, the big brown tent, the preachers who heralded forth so strongly the Second Coming of Christ, the Judgment, and men's accountability to God. I had a feeling of condescension as I thought of those sincere but unlearned men. They knew nothing of biblical criticism. Even so, it was under their honest preaching that I joined the church and entered the Christian ministry.

My watch dial showed 2 a.m. when I broke away from the reminiscences, walked to the door and knocked. There was no answer. I knocked again, but still no response. The night was strangely still and silent. I knocked a third time, and called, but with no better results. Where could my parents be? I was sure they would have notified me if they had left town for some reason. After knocking and calling for the fourth time, I walked around to the bedroom window and called. When there was no answer, a vague un-easiness stole over me; I knew in my heart that something was amiss.

As I walked into the front yard, I could not shake the strong conviction that something strange had happened. For the first time, I noticed that it was a starless night, the stars apparently hidden by the brightness of the moon. A realization began to creep over me that this night which was almost as bright as day was also a night filled with a strange presence. An overwhelming power that made me feel uneasy seemed to be all around me. I had never seen such a night! A night without stars or sound—just brightness. A night suddenly charged with some awesome, intangible power that stole over my mind and body. My head whirled.

I tried to analyze my feelings, but I seemed to be under the hypnotic control of this strange night. I found myself wanting to strike out with my fists or cry out at the silence. But there was nothing to strike and no cry came from my lips.

I gazed into the heavens without a word, without a movement. I was fully conscious, but I almost fancied that I was dreaming. With an almost hypnotic stare, I gazed at the moon. The more I contemplated the heavens, the more uneasy I felt. With all the willpower that I could muster and with exercise of considerable physical effort, I broke from this strange power. I felt startled and very much alarmed. Why did I gaze? There was nothing to see but a moon. Why did I listen? There was nothing to hear. I decided to drive over to Uncle Joe's place to inquire about Dad and Mom.

The sound of my feet as I walked, the slamming of the car door, the noise of the motor—all seemed abnormally loud in this bright, silent night.

I drove the quarter of a mile to my uncle's place. There

15

the darkness of the house was not surprising, but I approached with a feeling of uncertainty, maybe a little fear.

As I walked from the car toward the house, I was nagged by the feeling that something was missing. What was so different here from my own home? I knocked, called and knocked some more, but no answer came. As I walked from the porch back toward the car, there came strongly to me again the feeling that some sight or sound was missing. Suddenly I knew: the dogs. Uncle Joe always kept a pen of hunting hounds. I should be hearing their barking.

A well-worn path of white sand took me to the pen. There I saw the dogs standing and looking upward, but not responding as I walked among them. They only moved out of my way, never ceasing to watch the heavens. Some of them whimpered, but there was no barking. It was as if their master had ascended into the heavens and they had seen him go. It seemed to me they were looking into an immeasurable distance. Then, as if their gaze were completed, they circled the pen, whimpered, and sought the security of the doghouse. Ignored and rejected by the dogs, I felt a childish wave of hurt and loneliness.

It was as if the intense silence was oppressing me with some vague message. My heart seemed to stop beating and my blood stilled its journey to assist me in listening. I fought again with this unnatural emotion and tried to pull myself back to reality. I could not imagine what fearful thing lurked in this beautiful, silent night, but it was terrifying. Getting quickly into my car, I felt as if I had found the embrace of a friend. I turned on the radio to find a refuge from the silence.

I can never outlive the memory of what I heard. The announcer's words tumbled and fought for expression. The man made little sense. He wasn't talking, he was almost screaming. "People are missing. . . . State guards have

16

been called out. . . . Airplanes have crashed. . . . Car drivers have disappeared. . . . Graves have opened. . . ."

I turned off the radio. For the first time, I feared that I knew the answer. I felt sick. Could this be it? Could it be what the old-timers called the Rapture? As a child, I had dreamed about it. If I did wrong, I feared Christ's coming. But at Church University I had learned better. There would be no physical resurrection or a rapture of the Christians. Could Church University have been wrong? Could the old-timers have been right? Could it be that Christ had really come? Could He have come tonight?

I had to have the answer. There was one way to know the truth. The facts were not to be found at Church University nor in a textbook that some learned scholar had written. I headed north to a little country cemetery where my grandparents had been buried. If the Rapture had occurred, their graves would be open. I knew that in a country cemetery I would find the explanation of this night's maddening mystery.

As I turned into the cemetery, I was fearful of what I might find. I am not sure that I was even breathing as my headlights slashed the darkness and illuminated the graves. Many were open. A weakness and numbness engulfed me as I walked toward our family plot.

I knew what I would find—and I was right. The graves of my grandparents were open.

There was no longer any mystery. The Rapture had taken place. This explained the random opening of the graves that I had seen earlier. It also explained why they seemed to have been opened from the inside. The cemeteries were not being moved; only some of the occupants were on the move. They had gone to the Marriage Supper of the Lamb.

O dear God! How could I have been so wrong? How many students had I destroyed through glorifying doubt

17

and asking meaningless questions of young and unin-
formed minds? As I stood by those open graves, I lived
through a nightmare of dread and fear.

I don't know how long I stood in the old cemetery,
but I remember that it was daylight when I turned toward
my car. I found the exit blocked. The cemetery and the
road were filling with people. All around me they were crying, staring, and screaming; they pointed to graves and
motioned toward the sky.

Almost on impulse, I began to wander among the
people. Here and there little groups stood pale and speechless around an unopened grave. What could they say? I
could imagine their thoughts. Sometime earlier a loved one
had joined the church, attended services, but had never
been converted. When he died, the minister spoke of his
good life and left the impression that he had gone to be
with Jesus. But the deceased had never been born again;
now the unopened grave gave mute testimony to his lostness.


It must have been 9:00 in the morning before the
crowd dispersed enough for me to drive back toward town.
It was as if my memory were driving for me. Without
thinking I turned left and then took a right turn toward the
little church on the corner. I could remember when the
grounds were filled with people and a tent had to be used
to accommodate the annual revival attendance. But that
had been so long ago. For years the attendance had been
so small that the church was almost nonexistent. There
would never again be the crowds of the old days.

How wrong I was. As I turned toward the church, the
streets were filled. It was necessary to park a block away.
As I walked to the church, it struck me for the first time.
There were no small children! There had been none with
their parents at the cemetery. What a world without little

18

children! Never again would I hear the laughter of a child or see the innocence of a baby's face.

As I pushed my way into the churchyard, I came face-to-face with my cousin Matthew Hyde. His face was pale, his eyes haunted, his lips tight in fear. When he spoke it was only to ask, "You, too, Steve?" The words burned into my brain. I knew only too well their meaning.

At a distance, moving through the crowd I saw my uncle Tim Chandler. He had been faithful in church attendance but had never been converted. His duties on the state's Supreme Court held first priority in his life, so much so that he had never married.

Someone started a song in the church. Those of us in the yard who were unable to get inside tried to join in. We had sung the song many times—"Oh, How I Love Jesus." The tragedy was that we had never really meant it.

When I left, the crowd was still a mass of talking, crying, praying people. Somehow the words of a half-forgotten sermon came back to me: "After the Rapture—What?" I never thought I would have to answer that question.

I drove back to my parents' home. The house was still quiet as death as I forced my way in through a window. The family room was on the right side of the hall that divided the old farmhouse. There the fireplace was still warm and filled with dying embers. On the mantel I saw Dad's glasses and on a table by his chair lay his Bible, opened to Matthew 24. I used to tease Dad about taking the Bible so literally. Now he was raptured to be with the Christ whom he trusted while I was left behind. The words of my cousin continued to stab my conscience: "You, too, Steve?" I felt a tightening in my throat.

With some hesitation but feeling compelled, I walked into my parents' bedroom knowing that it would be empty. The bedclothes lay in loose folds just as though Mother

19

and Dad were still in bed. I could see where their heads had made an imprint in the pillows.

I could stay in the house no longer. Maybe outside my tortured mind could find some relief from the agony of my loss.

Behind the home stood an old log building that had at one time served as a smokehouse. Scattered around it were gnarled and dying apple trees. For some reason I felt an urge to walk past the smokehouse and through the trees. I found myself almost running through the old orchard as if trying to escape the reality of the present. But how could I? I sought refuge in my yesterdays, but the memories of childhood could not stem the tide of doom that swept over me.

As I wandered back toward the house, I stopped. I could not bear any longer the sense of despair that gripped me. Under an old apple tree I dropped on my knees and prayed. I had spoken thousands of prayers in my lifetime, but never had I tried to pray in a world so completely in the grip of Satan. My prayer was short:

"Dear God, I have questioned the teachings of the Bible. In my self-deceit I have destroyed others. Forgive me, O God! Have mercy on my soul, and I will serve Thee even though it means death for me."

I arose and walked back toward the house knowing that to be a Christian in the Tribulation would mean just that—death in a world ruled by Satan incarnate in "the Beast." I shivered as I voiced aloud this name for the Antichrist given in the Revelation. My prayer for salvation rang in my ears like a death knell. I had been careless in my interpretation of the Scriptures, but I knew what they taught. Very clearly I could read my death warrant: "As many as would not worship the image of the beast should be killed" (Rev. 13:15).

Even with proof beyond reasonable doubt that the

Rapture had occurred, I cried out for evidence that these happenings were unreal. I turned to the television for hope. By now it was time for the noon world report.

I should have known that these events demanded special coverage, but I was in such a state of shock that I could not fully accept and organize what was happening. When I turned on the television, I discovered that a worldwide news special had been in progress since four o'clock in the morning.

The reports from around the world were monotonous with sameness: open graves, missing people, general chaos. There was one announcement, however, that was of special interest to me. Dr. Goldbar, prime minister of Germany, would give a special report to the world at 1 p.m. Since the nations of the world had formed an alliance with Germany, Dr. Goldbar was the one man whom the world population knew and would follow in this time of turmoil. Maybe he could bring some order out of this pandemonium. It was also reported that there would be a religious interpretation of events by Bishop Costo of Europe and Dr. Martin Kennedy of the United States.

At 12:30 Cousin Matthew and his wife, June, came to my parents' house. June's eyes were red from weeping, her hair disheveled; her appearance was that of a tormented soul. In her hand she grasped a baby's blanket and pacifier. Matthew was pale and tight-lipped. He wore an expression of anguished despair.

Sobbing softly, June told me of attending a Christmas party in the church fellowship hall. They had enjoyed the evening, and near midnight she and Matthew went to the church nursery to pick up their baby. It was exactly 12:00 when the attendant handed them their six-months-old son, John. June recalled that she had kissed him and then hugged an empty blanket to her breast. John was gone! I will never forget her pleading cry.

21

"O God! My baby's gone and I can't go with him. I want my baby. I want my baby. Matthew! Steve! Oh! My baby!"

Matt and I had grown up together. We were roommates at Church University and had both studied for the ministry. His mind was sharp. There was nothing that he liked better than a debate. He would question, analyze, and challenge his teachers and fellow students on any Bible doctrine. I went along with him in the debate. I can see clearly now what happened. We questioned others until we demolished our own beliefs.

It was now almost 1:00 on Christmas Day. So much had happened in the last 12 hours since midnight that we hadn't thought of eating. June went to Mother's well-stocked kitchen and soon had sandwiches and coffee ready. We knew that we needed the nourishment, although no one really felt like eating.

We were eating when the special news report began. Prime Minister Goldbar was presented by Bishop Costo of the Council of Churches.

Without preliminaries, Dr. Goldbar moved into his subject.

"It is my duty to bring a report to a grief-stricken world. For some years Germany and the Common Market Nations of Europe have been involved in the study of subversive elements in the world religions. During this study Bishop Costo warned me that I should prepare for a deceitful power play by a segment of fanatical Christians. It was the belief of the bishop and his research team that this radical group would try to bring about a fictitious event they called 'The Rapture.' I was also warned that the group had perfected strange powers to perform other great and wonderful signs. The purpose of these so-called miracles was to bring the world under the domination of the Jews and the Christians.

"Anyone who examines the record will be convinced that there is neither love nor deliverance in the Christian religion. The man Jesus, who is supposed to have 'raptured' people by the 'trump of God,'[1] was arrested, tried, and put to death by His own people. He was condemned by their law, not the Roman laws. He was rejected by the religious leaders of His people. Those learned leaders were not divided in their determination that the man Jesus should die for the good of the people. If any doubt my word, the book of the Christians, the Bible, records this fact: 'When the morning was come, all the chief priests and elders of the people took counsel against Jesus to put him to death.'[2] The leaders of His own people concluded after a night of study that He must die for His crimes against the people.

"Our research council concluded that Jesus' followers would not give up. It was further discovered that they had made a threat to get even with the world for Jesus' death. They hid their spirit of revenge behind this so-called 'Rapture.' The true spirit of this radical group is found in the words of their major spokesman and philosopher, Paul: 'Jesus shall be revealed from heaven with his mighty angels, in flaming fire taking vengeance on them.'[3] Such an attitude is not one of forgiveness or love. It is just what Paul said—vengeance.

"Jesus' followers have done just what they threatened to do. They have taken revenge by bringing about the disappearance of millions. At the present, we don't know just how permanent this disappearance is. We don't know if it is real or feigned. It may be that they unearthed the bodies of their dead and have all gone into hiding. If Jesus has

---

1. 1 Thess. 4:16.
2. Matt. 27:1.
3. 2 Thess. 1:7-8.

23

returned, as some claim, neither He nor His disciples have been seen.

"This is the most heartless and evil act that the Christians have ever perpetrated. It was the Christians who burned Rome, and to this day they have tried to blame Nero. Because of crimes by Christ's followers, the Romans were forced to put many of them to death. They claimed, however, that they died for being good. Even today some talk of the 'purity' of the Christians.

"The Christians' Bible has one purpose; that is to defame the name and character of one whom I know personally. That thoughtful and benevolent person is called the Prince of This World. He seeks only the advancement of men. Look at the facts. The Christians' Bible has tried to discredit the Prince by attaching evil names to him and attributing evil acts and a vile nature to him. Is it evil to grow? To develop? To gain knowledge? Or seek to be as the gods? Again, look at the record. In the Christians' own book, the Prince was only encouraging man to reach for his ultimate potential. 'For, God doth know that in the day ye eat thereof, then your eyes shall be opened, and ye shall be as gods.'[4]

"The great Prince was only telling man that we have the potential for growth beyond Adam's imagination. Someone had to be the teacher and point the way. The Prince did not say to hate, to kill, or to be unkind. He only said, 'You have potential to be as gods. Do it!' It was the Prince who delivered Adam and Eve from Eden. If he had not done this, would you be living? Would man have walked on the moon? Would the world have the glory that it has today if naked people were still keeping the Garden of Eden?

"The Prince never asked for war with the Christians.

---

4. Gen. 3:5.

24

He believes in God as much as any follower of Christ. Did he not go before God and talk with Him as is recorded in the Book of Job in the Christians' Bible? The Prince is no atheist. This world is the kingdom of the Prince; and do not people fight to preserve their homeland? The Prince, however, went the second mile to preserve peace when Jesus came to the earth. Again the record is clear from the book of the Christians: 'My kingdom is not of this world.'[5] Jesus himself gave public testimony that this world was the kingdom of my friend when He referred to him as 'the prince of this world.'[6]

"May I repeat, the Prince never sought trouble with Jesus; he sought peace. Again, this may be found in the Christians' Bible: 'All these things [this part of the world] will I give thee, if thou wilt fall down and worship me.'[7] The Prince was willing to share his kingdom with Jesus in exchange for cooperation from Him. But was Jesus willing to cooperate? Were His followers willing to make any compromises? No! Christianity brought revolution to the world.

"The very coming of Jesus was deceitful. He came with the promise of 'peace, good will toward men.'[8] Did He bring peace? Did He bring goodwill? From the day of His birth to the present, the world has been divided over Him. After He was established on the earth, Jesus himself admitted that He had come to destroy and to bring discord: 'Think not that I am come to send peace on earth: I come not to send peace, but a sword. For I am come to set a man at variance against his father, and the daughter against her mother, and the daughter in law against her mother in law.'[9] My friends, these are words of revolution —and the exact words of Jesus.

------

5. John 18:36    6. John 14:30.    7. Matt. 4:9.    8. Luke 2:14.
9. Matt. 10:34-35.

"Today, Jesus and His Christians have brought the world to its greatest sorrow and tragedy. Mothers are crying for babies who have disappeared. Husbands are brokenhearted over wives who are gone. Families are in utter turmoil. The Christians' Bible tried to present Jesus as a savior, a peacemaker, and as one who loves. If this is true, why has He brought such sorrow to a kingdom that is not His?

"Jesus said that He was a savior. What has He saved you from? Sickness? Death? Sorrow? Hunger? No! All of His promises have been directed to some nebulous world yet to come.

"I cannot undo the sorrow brought by the disappearance of your loved ones. I can, however, promise you that with your help and cooperation it will never happen again. I promise you a world of pleasure. Jesus and His followers taught, 'Thou shalt not.' I can promise freedom from want, in a world of prosperity unequaled in all history. Follow me and I will not disappoint you. I will make your life one of joy, happiness, and peace.

"My friends, I share in your sorrow of losing loved ones in the evil separation of this so-called 'Rapture.' My heart goes out to every broken home. I extend a hand of support and assurance to every heart touched by fear. What has been done by the Christians cannot be undone. However, with your cooperation we will once and for all bring an end to the Christians' reign of terror. Under the leadership of Bishop Costo, we will worship one who has promised man pleasure and full freedom. He gives happiness in the life to be lived now—not some mythical world to come. This earth belongs to the Prince, and with your help, we will make his kingdom glorious and fulfilling for all.

"All citizens will be kept informed on the mysteries of the disappearance of your loved ones as the information

26

comes in. You will receive full reports as the steps are taken to free the world forever from the tyranny of the Christians.

"I bid all citizens 'Good night,' and may the spirit of the Prince of This World guide us all."

It seemed ages before one of us even moved. What the others thought, I don't know. For me, the truth was as old as Genesis. In the beginning, the words of God had been distorted by Satan to rob Adam and Eve of the Garden of Eden, but never had the Scriptures been so twisted as they had been today. Satan was still vilifying the truth and leading men to believe a lie.

The voice of the announcer brought me back to the present. "All citizens are advised to stand by for a major announcement by the prime minister of France."

The announcement was short. "Citizens of the world. The 10 members of the Common Market Nations of Europe are in no way dissolving their governments. But I am authorized by these governments to announce that Dr. Judas Goldbar is of this date the Prime Minister of the United States of Europe."

It seemed unbelievable. This was an announcement of the revival of the old Roman Empire, as many scholars believe the Bible predicts.

Before the three of us could begin a conversation, Bishop Costo and Dr. Martin Kennedy were presented for a joint statement which was read by Bishop Costo. He announced the organization of a World Church under the joint leadership of Bishop Costo in Europe and Dr. Martin Kennedy in the United States. The World Church, it was stated, would give its full backing to Dr. Goldbar as Prime Minister of the United States of Europe. They would support his efforts to unite the world and assuage the fear caused by the radical Christians with their vengeful "Rapture." An all-out emphasis would be given to the preaching

27

of a social gospel that would bring peace, contentment, and prosperity to all men who would live for this world.

For the next few minutes I sat staring at the television screen. But the pictures were those on the screen of my mind. I saw a small boy in Sunday school, a teenager preaching, a young man with dreams of spending his life in the Christian ministry. Then I saw a man who had sold his dreams because of pride; he now sat forlorn and hopeless. Somewhere I had surrendered my faith, and, in the process, I had missed the Rapture.

When I turned to speak to Matt and June, it was almost as if I were an actor watching a play in which I played a major role. Even when I spoke, it was as if I stood by listening and watching myself.

"We know from the Scriptures what this means. We're facing seven years of the Tribulation. It's obvious that Prime Minister Goldbar is the Beast, and Bishop Costo is the False Prophet. It is only a matter of time until their real natures will emerge. The question is, What are we to do?"

Neither Matt nor June moved. Matt was holding a cup of coffee, now cold, and staring out a window. June seemed to be looking through the wall.

The words of Jesus pounded through my thinking: "For then shall be great tribulation, such as was not since the beginning of the world" (Matt. 24:21). I thought, How tragic it is for me to be here. If opportunity could save a man, I would have been saved a thousand times.

While the fire slowly exchanged its glow of red for a coat of gray, we sat in the silence of a terrible dread. My gaze joined that of Matt. We watched the sun sink from sight, the shadows of the trees creep across the yard, and the cattle stand with bowed heads. From our childhood the scene had been a symbol of peace, but the contentment of childhood was now supplanted by fear of our tomorrows. This world was quickly moving into the clutches of the Beast. What a change by one brief event called the Rapture!

There are times when all men need to escape from their thoughts, when to think is to suffer pain. To look at Matt and June was to read a completed tragedy at a glance. To look at the burned out fire was to see our future, gray and dead. How does one face the future in a world controlled by Satan himself? The years to come had already been recorded in the Bible. In our world men would hate, kill, suffer, curse God, and worship Satan with abandon.

"Matt." The sound of my voice was like that of a stranger. "We've got to take some action, do something, prepare for the future. We can't just sit here!"

"True, Steve, true," was his detached reply. Then for the first time a spark of humor blended with irony found its way into our conversation.

"You know, Steve, you're quoting from the preachers and their old 'brown tent revival' theology. That's the kind of beliefs we gave up at Church University. You just said, 'We've got to take some action, do something, prepare for the future.' It sounds like one of the old boys preaching on 'Prepare to Meet Thy God.'"

"That's just it, Matt. This earth has an appointment with an evil personality, the Beast. We're left here for that meeting. What are we going to do about it?"

June made a practical suggestion. "Boys, I'm hungry. Don't you think dinner would help our planning?"

We agreed that hungry and tired people could never make sound decisions. We had eaten only a sandwich since the past midnight, and could hardly believe that we had been sitting here since the 1 p.m. report. It would be best to eat and then talk.

As June prepared dinner, Matt and I rebuilt the fire and watched the news. Over and over the chaotic state of the world was pictured, but each dark problem was presented as having found its solution in Prime Minister Goldbar. It was unbelievable that one man could have the world so completely in his hands. He had risen to power so quickly and so absolutely that his authority had to be satanic. When the announcer presented world economic problems, he always followed through by stating, "But Prime Minister Goldbar has presented the following solution: . . ." For every ill, Goldbar was the great physician.

June soon had us sitting down to Christmas dinner. Mother had roasted a turkey, baked pies and a cake on Christmas Eve. We ate, but it was a forced, mechanical activity. There was no holiday mood. As I ate a piece of the special Christmas cake that Mother always baked for me, I felt a deep yearning to see my parents. I missed them terribly, but I was glad that they did not have to face the future of seven years under the Beast. The thought came to me that while we were eating Christmas dinner in a somber atmosphere, Mother and Dad were enjoying the Marriage Supper of the Lamb.

# 2

# Deceitful Whiteness

*I saw, and behold a white horse: and he that sat on him had a bow; and a crown was given unto him* (Rev. 6:2).

With dinner over and a big fire burning, we all knew that the time for decision making was upon us. June presented an idea that started us in the direction which we took. I am sure it saved our lives. She said, "Steve, Dad wrote a book entitled *Living Through the Tribulation*. He understood that the first three and a half years would be a time of peace because the Antichrist would need that much time to consolidate his kingdom."

"June," I replied, "I recall a sermon your father preached in which he said that in the beginning of Antichrist's reign a treaty would be signed between Israel and the world kingdom of Antichrist. However, he also said that after three and a half years the treaty would be broken and world peace would be ended. He gave as his proof Daniel 9:27: 'And he shall confirm the covenant with many for one week: And in the midst of the week he shall cause the sacrifice and the oblation to cease.'"

"If that's true," Matt added, "we have three and a half years to prepare a hideaway and store supplies."

I responded, "If that's the timetable, don't you think we should stay here on the farm and prepare for the Beast, the Tribulation, and Armageddon?" My comment was more an expression of hope than a question, but we agreed that this seemed feasible.

For a few days we lived a trance-like life—eating, sleeping, and talking. We seemed unable to come to grips with the future. But on New Year's Day as we listened to the news, we were shocked back into activity. What we heard came right out of the Bible.

"The major news story at the beginning of the year is one of peace and goodwill. Prime Minister Goldbar has signed a treaty with Israel, Egypt, the Communist nations, Japan, and all the Western world to cooperate in a one-world of religious peace and economic prosperity. The economic program will be coordinated from Berlin under the direct supervision of Prime Minister Goldbar. The religious and educational programs will be under the direction of Bishop Costo in Rome. He will represent all the world's religions. We can look forward to prosperity and peace."

The broadcast concluded with an announcement that Prime Minister Goldbar and Bishop Costo would have a special New Year's telecast for the world at 10 p.m.

I remember clearly the broadcast made the world wild with joy. Prime Minister Goldbar promised a job for everyone. Plans for rebuilding the Temple in Jerusalem were only the beginning of a worldwide construction program. From the World Bank in Berlin, projects in every nation would be funded. The programs would be financed by each government contributing five percent of its annual gross income. Because of the economic and military potential of this program, it was reported that a treaty involving all the nations on earth was being signed. This organization was to be known as the Alliance of the World, and it would be under the advisory leadership of Prime Minister Goldbar. Berlin was announced as the international headquarters.

When Prime Minister Goldbar had completed his speech, Bishop Costo appeared on the screen. He was introduced as the new chairman of the Committee for Religon, Education, and Health for the Alliance of the World. Here were the two most powerful men on earth. All of my life I had heard about the coming Antichrist. Now I had seen and heard him along with the False Prophet.

Near midnight on that New Year's Day, Matt, June, and I were able with some degree of calmness to plan for the future. We agreed that a well-concealed hideaway must be found and that it must be stocked with supplies for a long stay. About two miles from my parents' home was an abandoned coal mine where my father had worked many years ago. If the mine were safe and dry, this would be the perfect place.

At nine o'clock the next morning, the three of us made our way across the pastures and woods toward the old mine. In about an hour we reached the entrance. We had to force our way through the trees, undergrowth, and tall weeds that stood as silent sentinels guarding the opening. It seemed as if nature resented the gaping wounds made by the miners and she was trying to hide the ugly scars. How fortunate for us that much of the low growth was cedar, which stays green the year round.

Standing in the mouth of the mine, we exclaimed almost as one person, "This is perfect!" The supporting cedar timbers were still sound; the floor was dry. No one lived close and there were no roads or trails that came this way. From my parents' home we could bring supplies without detection. Our exploration of the old mine convinced us that some hard work would give us a place to live during the last three and a half years of the Tribulation.

As we returned home, for the first time since the Rapture we talked and planned with some hope.

Three years passed quickly, years of hard labor. During the winter months Matt and I slipped away to work in the mine. A door strong enough to keep out intruders was of prime importance. It was built of a double thickness of oak and set into stone and cement walls three feet thick. Living and storage areas were built. We found a spring of water, dug a drainage ditch, and prepared sanitation areas. A second door, small and well hidden at the rear of our storage room, could be used if escape were ever necessary.

We used different routes in our trips to the mine in order to avoid developing paths that might later lead to our detection.

From early morning until night during the spring, summer, and fall, Matt and I farmed while June preserved, dried, and canned food for use during the three and a half years of starvation and death that were to come. How grateful she was for mother's adequate supply of canning essentials.


Months and years melted together for us. We had agreed that we could slip away into hiding more easily if we were not known. I had been away from home for many years, and knew very few people in the community. Also our farm being outside the little town helped. There were no visits, and we never stopped to talk with anyone when we occasionally purchased supplies. We had no mailing address. I continued paying utility bills, which were still in my father's name.

It wasn't difficult to remain isolated even in so small a community. The people had never been so prosperous and seemed to have no concern for others. Money and pleasure were to be had with ease. The townspeople like the rest of the world, seemed bent on drinking deeply from the cup of sinful pleasure.

The nations were united economically, religiously, and socially. From his headquarters in Germany, Prime Minister Goldbar received praise from around the globe. His scientific research had found cures for cancer and most heart diseases. With fear of these major physical illnesses alleviated and with unprecedented prosperity, the world worshiped at the altar of pleasure. They loved Goldbar. His military power seemed unnecessary.

As I mused over the state of the world with Goldbar as its absolute head, I knew that a crisis was at hand. Three years had passed since the Rapture. It would be only a short time before a worldwide move would be made to consolidate and insure the power of the Alliance of the World.

On a Sunday night we were sitting in front of the old home fireplace. Many times in the past Matt and I had played here. Tonight, however, we were not in a jovial mood. We had just read Revelation 13 for our evening devotions. Our discussion centered around verses 16-17: "And he causeth all, both small and great, rich and poor, free and bond, to receive a mark in their right hand, or in their foreheads: and that no man might buy or sell, save he that had the mark, or the name of the beast, or the number of his name." The three of us knew that we would eventually be faced with a legal demand to take that mark as a symbol of our loyalty to the world government.

I remember well my thoughts that evening. How many times I had ridiculed my students for taking the Revelation as a book of facts. It was absurd to believe there could be a personal Antichrist. But now I had seen him and heard him.

I believe that I can recall verbatim my comments that night:

35

"Matt, we've been farming and working at the mine for over three years. Goldbar is at the pinnacle of his world power. Now, if June's father was right in his prediction of events, the time of peace indicated in the first seal in Rev. 6:1-2 is almost over. We must be prepared to go into hiding at any moment."

Matt's rejoinder suggested a deep sorrow.

"Steve, if we had earlier possessed half the faith that we have now, we would have been raptured and not headed for a coal mine." I could only nod my head in silent agreement.

For weeks the news reports had hinted at the discontent of some nations with the food distribution. The more heavily populated nations brought charges before the delegates to the Alliance of the World. They alleged that the food distribution was based upon the wealth of the nations and not upon the population.

After lengthy debates, it was the genius of Prime Minister Goldbar that solved the dilemma. He recommended that every person in the world be given a computer-based number which was to be tattooed on the right hand. "Economic Mark" was the legal name given to the number. Goldbar further stated that the Food Administrator of the Alliance would buy all the food and distribute it to the nations of the world according to population. Only the nations and people loyal to the leadership of the Alliance would be permitted to buy or sell.

This program was acclaimed by the world. The Senate of the United States fully approved. Senator Esther Canady stated, "I am so concerned about the needy of the world that I will be glad to have my Alliance number recorded not only on my hand but also on my forehead."

Within 12 hours after the United States had approved the world number, it was announced that all citizens must have their Social Security numbers recorded on the right hand. This would be done by the Department of Internal Revenue. Citizens would have 30 days in which to comply with the order. They could report to any federal building or post office with their Social Security card, and the number would be imprinted permanently on the right hand, or, following Senator Canady, on the forehead.

If there had ever been any doubt concerning Antichrist and his kingdom, it was erased. We were there. The Alliance of the World was the empire of Antichrist, the Beast. Goldbar was the Antichrist and Bishop Costo was the False Prophet. The economic number was the Mark of the Beast recorded in Rev. 19:20.

The smoothness with which Goldbar gained power was amazing. It seemed that everything he did was for the good of all men. Who could object to a hungry world being fed? Who would not approve an economic program that brought prosperity to all nations? Who could object to an organized effort to identify the population of each nation so that adequate food would be distributed to all? What man or woman would voice disapproval of a health program that had brought an end to such dreaded diseases as cancer and heart attack? The world had needs. Prime Minister Goldbar was meeting these needs so swiftly and adequately that satanic genius had to be helping him. Could anyone wonder that he was applauded as the savior of the world?

Matt and I decided that it was time for us to go into hiding. And we were almost ready. So much had already been moved that the final task could be accomplished with only a few trips. We had never used a truck or tractor in moving for fear of attracting attention and leaving obvious tracks that might lead to the mine. We had used horses, feeling that with so many hoofprints in the pasture our moving would not be detected. All the trips had been made at night.

It was midnight when we loaded four horses for the last trip. As we left the yard, each step filled the air with sounds of loneliness. The soft thud of the horses' hoofs sounded melancholy in the gloom of the night. I had never felt so depressed.

By daylight all signs of the final move were erased and the horses were driven into the backside of the pasture. We had prepared the best we could for the seige of the Beast.

The world had never had a ruler like Goldbar. For three and half years the man had made no mistakes. Paul's description was perfect: "Even him, whose coming is after the working of Satan with all power" (2 Thess. 2:9).

From the time of the Rapture there had been over three years of hard work for us. But now that we were in hiding, we were involved in the hardest test of all: waiting. But waiting for what?

Within a week our coal mine home was in order. One of the offshoot tunnels had been completely blocked and paneled. This was quarters for Matt and June. I had similar quarters on the opposite side of the main entrance. Food, clothing, medicine, and fuel were stored in sufficient quantity for years. Two television sets, one electric and one battery powered; also two radios were among the supplies. The power lines to the old coal mine were easily repaired. It had been a simple matter to run wire underground from the old mine office to our new home. We even rigged up an outside antenna in a tree in such a way that it was camouflaged.

June remembered to bring a calendar which would serve for the next several years. It was pocket-sized, which proved to be a valuable feature considering what lay ahead for us.

We had been in the mine for two weeks when a routine evening newscast was interrupted with an unbelievable announcement that Prime Minister Goldbar had been assassinated. He had been shot by an Israeli as he had left his headquarters in Berlin. The assailant had been killed immediately, but there was speculation of a worldwide conspiracy. Throughout the world Jews and Christians were being arrested. The military power of Israel was readied for national defense even as her defense minister stated that he knew nothing of the assassination. He emphasized the appreciation Israel had for Prime Minister Goldbar; it was only through the Alliance of the World under the prime minister's leadership that Israel had been able to rebuild the Temple and reinstitute offering of the Mosaic sacrifices. Since Israel had signed a seven-year peace and economic treaty with the Alliance, she had enjoyed a building program in housing and industry unparalleled in the history of the nation.

There was no world leader to take the prime minister's place. One reporter stated that many nations had declared a state of emergency and were fearful of civil war.

The second day after Goldbar's assassination we listened to a special bulletin from the World Peace Bureau, the secret police of the Alliance:

"A citizen of Israel, Joseph Dion, age 32, has been named as the assassin of Prime Minister Judas Goldbar. Joseph Dion was a member of an extremist group who refused to accept the Economic Mark of the Alliance. This group calls the symbol 'the Mark of the Beast.' They refer to Prime Minster Goldbar as 'the Beast,' and to Bishop Costo as 'the False Prophet.' These radicals have conspired to destroy the World Alliance. Joseph Dion, although a Jew, attended secret meetings of another radical group called Tribulation Christians."

The announcer reported an emergency session of the Senate of the Alliance of the World, and that additional

39

information on the assassination would be given as soon as possible.

Before the reporter finished, the program was interrupted with a special news bulletin.

"The Senate of the Alliance of the World has taken emergency action against a group of rebellious religious fanatics. All world governments have concurred with this decision. All people who do not have the Economic Mark are enemies of the Alliance of the World government. A 30-day grace period will be given in which they may receive the mark. Those who do not comply will be put to death as enemies of the state."

At the end of the Senate report, all listeners were advised that Bishop Costo would have an important announcement at 11:45.

At the appointed time the three of us were listening and watching. Bishop Costo appeared in full religious garb. He appeared calm and confident.

"Citizens of the world. The entire globe has been saddened by the news of the death of our beloved leader, Prime Minister Judas Goldbar. But there is no reason for sadness or fear. Our leader is more than a man. He is divine, the savior of the world. Some of you may doubt this, but I will now present evidence to you that Prime Minister Goldbar is supernatural.

"In my hand I hold a letter entrusted to me by the prime minister. He requested that this letter should be read to the world in the event of his death. The statement is concise. It reads as follows: 'I came as the savior of the world. Evil men have tried to prevent my good works. If I die, I will arise on the third day at 12 noon.'"

Bishop Costo continued, "It is five minutes before 12 on the third day. I will now take you by television to the next room where Prime Minister Goldbar's body lies in state."

40

The cameras brought in a clear picture of the flag of the Alliance of the World and the flags of all the nations of the earth. Honor guards stood at attention. The president of the United States, the prime minister of England, the prime minister of Russia, and the heads of many other nations were standing by the unopened casket. It was now exactly 12:00.

Slowly the lid of the ornate casket began to open. At first, I assumed that it was controlled by some electronic device. There had been no report as to the location of the wound that had killed Goldbar, but now it was plain. An effort had been made to cover the wound, but one could see that the right side of the head had suffered extreme damage. There lay Dr. Goldbar, pale and lifeless. How the mighty had fallen!

What happened next was incredible. With the whole world as a witness, Bishop Costo stepped to the casket and said, "Savior of the world, I say to you, Arise from your sleep!"

With the utmost confidence Bishop Costo reached into the casket and took the hand of Prime Minister Goldbar. I saw the death pallor and lifelessness yield to the blush of health. With the strength of an athlete, Goldbar stepped from the casket. Guards fainted, heads of state turned pale and moved quickly out of camera range. News reporters ran.

Bishop Costo stepped to the microphone. "Citizens, it is my privilege to present to you the risen savior of the world. All men must worship him. Those who do not are the enemies of the Alliance and of the savior of the world."[1]

_____

1. The Bible says, "The coming of the lawless one will be in accordance with the work of Satan displayed in all kinds of counterfeit miracles, signs, and wonders" (2 Thess. 2:9, NIV).

As Goldbar stepped to the microphone, I could see a scar on the right side of his head. There was no other sign of physical problem. The hurt was healed. When he spoke, his voice was clear and strong.

"Fellow citizens, I was resurrected by the power of the Prince of This World. It is my privilege to bring peace and prosperity, and to make it possible for all to enjoy the pleasures of this world. We should all live in peace."

I had heard Goldbar make many speeches. He was always pleasant and understanding. But now, just for a moment, I saw the flicker of satanic hate flit across his face as he said, "We cannot permit any unbelieving, fanatical groups to rob the world of pleasure and prosperity. Those who seek to do so are the enemies of all men, and they shall die."

Then he quickly added, "But there is no reason why anyone should deny himself the glories of this kingdom. As the resurrected leader of the world, I come with love and goodwill for all. The nation of Israel and some radical Christians have not accepted the Economic Mark. From this time on, no one will be excused. Police and advisors will be sent from Germany to each capital of the world to see that the law requiring the Economic Mark is strictly enforced."

Goldbar and Costo had simply served notice on the world that the day of grace was over. Even though I was sitting in the warmth of the coal mine, I suddenly felt a chill creep over my whole body. It was not Dr. Goldbar's speech that chilled me. It was the sudden realization that he had been resurrected on Easter Sunday.

Another special report was announced for Wednesday. These announcements were now becoming a regular part of life. Wednesday at 7 a.m., along with the rest of the world, we three were listening. The program was short and to the point. Prime Minister Goldbar stated,

"During the hours of my death I was in the presence of the Prince of This World. Those who have been taught in the so-called Christian religion will remember that even the man Jesus of Nazareth admitted that the Prince of the World was in control of this earthly kingdom.[2] The spirit of the Prince of This World now lives within me. Through his goodness I have been given all power. The world is mine. There can be no war. I am the savior of the world. There can be no false religions. As of this day all armies of the world and all national leaders shall answer to me for their conduct.

"On behalf of the only true church, the World Church, I declare that Bishop Costo is the only true priest. Those who defy this true church shall not live. However, I do not seek nor wish harm to anyone. Worship the Prince and live. Follow the Prince and be happy.

"If you were reared in the Christian faith, you know that I am the chosen one to be the light of the world in its hour of darkness. The Bible speaks of me as 'Lucifer, son of the morning.'[3] Lucifer means 'light-bearer.' I am resurrected as the light of the world.

"Ezekiel prophesied of me; and I would remind you that Ezekiel stated that his knowledge came from God when he wrote of me: 'Thou sealest up the sum, full of wisdom, and perfect in beauty. Thou hast been in Eden the garden of God; every precious stone was thy covering. . . . Thou art the anointed cherub that covereth, and I have set thee so: thou wast upon the holy mountain of God; thou hast walked up and down in the midst of the stones of fire. Thou wast perfect.'[4]

"If God called me 'perfect' and 'anointed' and 'full of

---

2. Matt. 4:8-9.
3. Isa. 14:12.
4. Ezek. 28:12-15.

43

wisdom,' why will misguided people reject me and seek to prevent the will of God from being carried out here on the earth? I do not ask that anyone do more or less than Michael the archangel. When we confronted each other, he 'durst not bring against [me] a railing accusation.'[5] The archangel knew my power. He recognized that the world is mine and that it was futile for him to fight against me. For one to deny my rights on the earth and to stand against me is to deny God and to stand against Him. I am the Prince of This World.

"I will be 'like the most High'[6] here upon the earth. I will 'exalt my throne.'[7] I am 'perfect' and 'full of wisdom.' I am the 'anointed cherub' to rule the earth. I was 'in Eden the garden of God.' I am the rightful ruler because God said, 'I have set thee so.'

"World citizens, let God work through me to give us a better world. Let there be no hate, bitterness, or unkindness. I forgive the one who tried to destroy me. I forgive those who worked with him. I forgive them 'for they know not what they do.'

"However, I must establish my kingdom upon the earth. The will of God must be done. I have come as the savior of the world, and I must do the work that is mine.

"Good night! And may the spirit of the Prince of This World be with you."

"What a genius!—but what a distorter of the Scriptures," June said sadly. "He took them from their setting, and never mentioned that the description of him as 'perfect' was made before he fell."

No one felt like replying. It was staggering and sobering to see the prophecies fulfilled right before our eyes.

---

5. Jude 9.
6. Isa. 14:14.
7. Isa. 14:13.

Spring and summer passed and gave way to fall. It was a little surprising when June suggested Christmas decorations. There could be no gaity, but if ever we realized the importance of Christ's coming to earth, it was this year.

On Christmas morning we read together Luke's Christmas story. It held special meaning for the three fugitives seeking survival in a world ruled by Satan incarnate.

We had been advised of a special report to be given on Christmas Day from the Senate of the Alliance of the World. I began to wonder just how many times we had heard these official reports. But even so, we eagerly awaited each announcement.

As usual, Bishop Costo appeared first. He presented the prime minister of France to speak for the heads of the nations and for the Senate of the World Alliance. As the television cameras brought the great halls of the Alliance into the living rooms of the earth, no one could fail to be impressed. Never had the heads of so many nations congregated in one room. There were flags familiar and unfamiliar: one was new and ominous. The Alliance flag was white, and on it was the face of a beast with 10 horns.

I lost interest in the flags as the prime minister of France began to speak.

"Citizens of the world, it is my honored privilege to present to you the first and only great world leader. It is my high privilege by vote of all national governments and by vote of the Senate of the Alliance to crown Dr. Judas Goldbar PRINCE OF THIS WORLD—a true patriot, a lover of all men in one world."

There he stood—calm, smiling, and with an expression of utter kindness. When he spoke, I felt drawn to bow in the presence of one who seemed noble and filled with love. He appeared to be the personification of all goodness. We listened as he spoke.

"Citizens of one world, I accept this crown. But before I was chosen by nations to rule the world, I was chosen by one greater than man. During the days of my death I descended into the home of my lord, the Prince of This World. He has possessed me by his spirit and his power. I do no work of my own, but I do his works and his will. If you know me, Judas Goldbar, you know him who sent me. He lives in me. We are one. If you love me, you love him. To worship me is to worship him. I can do much for this world through his power, which will be used for the good of all men. Now the rulers of this world have voted me their prince. I am honored. My flag is white to symbolize the purity of my government. Upon the flag is the head of a strong beast to represent the power of the Alliance of the World. The beast has 10 horns in honor of the nations of the old Roman Empire that trusted me first and thereby brought me to this happy hour.

"The emblem of my government is a white horse with a rider holding a bow, but there are no arrows. The horse is to remind all men that I can move with power and swiftness. The bow throughout the history of man has been the mark of a warrior. The world must know that as Prince of This World I have power that cannot be challenged. However, I have chosen to have no arrows on my emblem because I come with peace and goodwill toward men. The motto of my kingdom is 'In the Prince We Trust.' My official title is 'Prince of This World.'"

I thought, How much in character it is for Goldbar to accept his crown on Christmas Day. Just another way of showing his contempt for Christ, and another effort to displace Him in the minds of the people.

I remember no more of the program, but I do recall thinking, This is crazy. It was almost as if some amateur writer were making a fifth-rated comedy out of the Book of Revelation. The white horse and rider had just been shown and explained on world television. There was no doubt in my mind that before his assassination Dr. Judas Goldbar had been used of Satan; but now he was Satan Incarnate. He was the Beast.

# 3

# The Death Warrant

*He went forth conquering, and to conquer* (Rev. 6:2).

Since we had been in hiding, we had not gone into town; it was dangerous to expose oneself. But we were all curious to know how the man of the street was taking these world changes. I decided to leave the mine before daybreak, walk back to the old farmhouse and from there go into town.

When I talked this over with Matt and June, they saw no real danger with one exception.

Matt asked, "Steve, what about the Mark of the Beast? What if you're asked why you don't have it?"

Before I could answer, June had the solution. "Since it's cold, why don't you wear gloves? If you think you may need to take them off, I can use black ink and counterfeit the mark."

We all paused. This was the first time that we had in a personal way faced the importance of the Economic Mark.

"No, June," I said. "I've compromised with the Christian faith and almost lost my soul. I can't hide behind even a false mark. I'll keep the gloves on."

It was cold and raining as I walked through the pasture toward the old home place. I was glad for the high boots to protect my clothes. Although we had been gone for several months, I found no evidence that anyone had been around the house.

It was 10:00 when I walked into the little town. I was in no way prepared for the changes that I saw. This small town of my birth had at one time been the shopping center for five coal-mining communities. But for years the mines had been closed, and the one street of stores had stood half empty.

As I crossed the railroad, it was obvious something unusual was going on. The town was filled with people. As I got closer, to my amazement I discovered the buildings were no longer empty. This was a boom town! But why? What had happened?

Because I had been gone most of the years since I left for college, I knew very few of the people. This made it possible to move about freely. No one paid any attention to me.

One place that I remembered well was John's Cafe. The place was full and talk was flowing freely. I sat at a corner table while I drank my coffee and watched and listened. Within a few minutes I learned that the major coal mines were reopened, some of which had been closed for 40 years. They discussed the new deep mining equipment now in use. Prosperity was here. Coal was being shipped around the world. Once again black gold was the world's major source of energy.

One thing that caught my attention was the picture of Prince Goldbar on the wall above the cash register. Why was it there? My answer came from a rough-looking coal miner and his friend sitting at a table next to mine.

"You know, Fred, we've never had it so good. There's the man who's saved the world." As he spoke he pointed

49

toward the picture. Goldbar looked much as he did on television. In this full length photograph, he was dressed in military uniform. He was a strong looking man with dark hair. He stood six feet tall and weighed approximately 190 pounds. His expression was that of a kind and understanding leader.

The miner continued: "I know my baby was stolen away by the Christians just like your wife was, Fred. There are some things that I don't understand about it, but I know this. I've got more money and my wife's been cured of cancer. Prince Goldbar's done this for me. As far as I know, he's done nothing evil to anyone. I'm for him and I believe he's of God. Wasn't he raised from the dead?

"I'll tell you something else, Fred. I've heard that there are some so-called Tribulation Christians hiding out here who won't take the World Economic Mark. For some crazy reason they call it the Mark of the Beast. The Mark has done us a lot of good. It was the Mark that opened the world markets for our coal. If I see any of these people hiding around here, I'll report them. I've never been so prosperous, and I intend to keep it that way."

I was beginning to feel uncomfortable and conspicuous since I was the only person present wearing gloves. I quickly found the correct change and quietly paid for the coffee as I left the cafe.

Every person whom I had seen had a number tattooed on the back of the right hand. Goldbar's control was becoming so complete that it would soon be impossible to buy a cup of coffee without showing the Economic Mark. How easily Satan had moved in. The very one who would destroy the world was esteemed today as the savior of all men.

Returning to my old home brought back floods of memories. As I walked past my uncle's empty house and on toward my father's deserted dwelling now blanketed by silence, I felt isolated and apart. Never before in my life had I felt so lonely. If I had not known the Scriptures and believed in the Rapture, I would have believed myself insane. Among the millions of people in a world there were only two others to my knowledge who believed as I. My Christian faith cut me off irrevocably from association with anyone except Matt and June. The world that I saw was a cruel, friendless one. It was three against the world.

The intense despondency enshrouding me became as poisonous tentacles that reached out to numb my body and deepen my dejection. Bewildered and disheartened I walked faster to get home.

My entire trip had taken less than four hours, but I was weary. The fatigue was not from physical exertion but from mental anguish. Each footstep and each memory attacked my tormented brain with one thought—"Three more years of the Beast." The world that I had known was lost forever.

Knowing that it would be my last visit to the old home, I moved deliberately and slowly. When I emerged through the back door, for some strange reason, I carefully closed and locked it. Why? Habit I suppose. My parents had been raptured. It would be too dangerous for me to return. The home of my youth must decay alone.

I again put on my boots which I had left when I went into town. As a boy, I used to sing as I walked with nature. But today I walked back to the mine depressed by the solitude. One does not sing as he walks from his home for the last time. And I was too near plagues, earthquakes, and famine for music.

"How was everything, Steve?" June and Matt asked the question in unison. It was really more than a question. There was a cry for hope in their tones. It was almost as if they were saying, "Steve, tell us that all of this is a terrible dream, that you found your parents, that our baby is at

51

home, and things are back to normal." How I too wished that I could awaken from all of this to find that it was only a bad dream! But I made an effort to be casual.

"You'd never know the old home town. Remember how half the buildings were empty? There's not one left vacant. The stores are filled with people. They've never been so prosperous. And do you know who's receiving all the credit? Prince Goldbar. His picture decorates the walls of businesses, and probably most of the homes. The people are making a god out of him.

"I overheard some disturbing conversation, too. Some of the men say there's a rumor that Christians are hiding out in this area. They say they'll report any who are found, even if the Chritians are members of their own families. It'll be too dangerous for us to venture into town again."

Silence reigned in our hideaway. We knew that we were trapped in our mine, threatened by the hot breath of the Beast of Revelation. Christians were the enemy. The Beast, Prince Goldbar, was the god of this world.

After my trip into town, our mood dropped to a new low. Conversation centered on one subject: the end of the world and our hope that we could survive the murderous last years of the Tribulation and make it into the Millennium. Food, entertainment, and comfort seemed unimportant. Eating was a necessity, but pleasure was unsought. Social standing, approval of the world, and material possessions that had received so much of our attention were now ignored completely. How our values had changed since the Rapture!

It seemed strange in the beginning of the Tribulation to find myself constantly thinking of survival. But now it had become the accepted thought pattern and center of our conversation. We were trying to prepare ourselves for the inevitable persecution. We knew that under the reign of the Beast slavery would be the norm. Death would be the major characteristic of his kingdom, and suffering would be his gift to all living.

On a Wednesday evening as we listened to the news we realized that Prince Goldbar was deeply involved in a death feud with all political and religious ideas that differed from his own. The announcement was a death sentence for us.

"Prince Goldbar reports that the World Peace Bureau has uncovered a plot by political dissenters. Tribulation Christians and other discontents plan to overthrow the world government. Because of this, a state of emergency has been declared. Anyone without the Economic Mark will be executed. If there are two witnesses who testify that a person is a political dissenter or a Tribulation Christian, such a person is to be executed immediately by the local government. Any group of 10 or more citizens may receive legal authority to organize a Vigilante Committee, bear arms, and carry out execution by contacting the Vigilante Committee, World Peace Bureau, Washington, U.S.A."

When I turned off the radio, I found myself smiling grimly. Not because I had heard anything funny, but because I knew that the Prince had made a big mistake. It may have been his first, but it proved to me that he was not infallible. With so much hate in the world, permission for vigilante committees to bear arms and to execute could only mean worldwide legalized murder. This proclamation would take peace from the world. The ruler who had posed as the prince of peace and goodwill would bring an uninhibited rampage of killing that was fearful to contemplate.

In retrospect, I will try to summarize this death blow to the Tribulation Christians and ultimately to the Jews.

Prince Goldbar began a propaganda campaign. When anything went wrong, he blamed the Christians. A food shortage developed in China, India, and Africa. Immediately Goldbar accused the Christians of poisoning the seed, the fertilizer, and the land. Pictures were shown of Christian men and women being captured in the fields. Next their confessions were published. It was not known until later that they had been tortured into giving false statements. The charges were made that Christians expected to gain control of the food market and use food supplies to gain control of the world.

Captured Christians were further compelled to confess that they were preparing for the Battle of Armageddon at which time Goldbar would be killed and they would take control of the world.

Part of Goldbar's propaganda included pictures of starving people standing outside a house looking in. Next, he showed pictures from inside the house of fat Christians eating from tables filled with choice foods. The propaganda machine was full of statements such as, "Common people are being forced into cannibalism while Christians grow fat and rich."

While the Tribulation Christians were portrayed as immoral and traitors to the state, Goldbar was presenting himself as holy and the savior of the world.

When an epidemic of cholera broke out in India, a dozen Tribulation Christian doctors were forced to confess over world television that they had contaminated the city water supplies, and infected the wells in rural areas. Many suspected that all of the confessions were false, but to a distressed world the Tribulation Christians were a convenient scapegoat.

The most telling propaganda was the accusation of a Christian conspiracy to rule the world. The rumor was that all the raptured Christians would return with Jesus Christ as the King. Prince Goldbar would be dethroned and Christ would be installed as King in Jerusalem. This rumor troubled Prince Goldbar and all the world's rulers.

He became hysterical when reference was made to a Millennial Kingdom. Some reported that his face became distorted with hate. He snarled like a fierce beast, and his eyes blazed with a maniacal vengeance.

During the early years of his reign, Goldbar had initiated laws that required all Christians to wear a badge with an emblem of a cross. The badge was worn on the outer garments and was clearly visible. During these early years it had not been illegal to be a Christian. If one were imprisoned, he was accused of illegal acts but not of a forbidden faith.

To prevent the Christians from accumulating money for espionage or war, heavy taxes were placed on them. In order to remain out of prison for failure to pay the taxes, many were forced to sell their homes, businesses, and personal belongings. It was understood that no loyal citizen would do business with Christians.

At the same time Goldbar held out an easy plan for any Christian to save himself from the tax and from prison. The only requirement was that he renounce his Christian faith, and pledge allegiance to the Alliance of the World. However, all who renounced their faith had to prove their sincerity by giving the names of five other Christians. As a reward for their renunciation and the naming of other Christians, the new citizen was given 10 percent of the estate of the betrayed Christians. All who professed faith in Christ were considered traitors. Therefore they had no right to own property. They were not guilty for being Christians; they were guilty for being traitors.

It became the order of the day to rob and murder Christians. Any citizen who found a family without the Economic Mark simply reported them or robbed them. The police and courts stood by in silence. If anyone tried to defend a Christian, he was in trouble with the world government. Christians had no rights in a world controlled by Prince Goldbar, and he had the backing of world governments and the people. Repeatedly Goldbar stated, "The good citizen is an alert citizen." By this he meant, "Alert to report Christians."

In the first years of the Tribulation everything was kept legal. It was not against the law to be a Christian. In practice, however, the Christian was fair game for any group, and they had no legal protection.

The next step was anticipated by most Tribulation Christians. Goldbar proclaimed that they could no longer be tolerated. In a speech he reported that they were plotting to overthrow his government.

"Christians talk constantly of a war of deliverance called Armageddon and of a new kingdom that they call the Millennium. Because of this all Christians are traitors and are sentenced to die. If one is a true citizen of the Alliance of the World, he will gladly take the Economic Mark. If he refused the mark, he is a Christian and a traitor. If the government of the Alliance is to survive, *all Christians must die!*

"If anyone has knowledge of a Christian and does not report him, he is guilty of treason and worthy of death. No man or woman can live in this kingdom and be a traitor. To be a Christian or to fail to report a Christian is traitorous." Thus, to be a Christian was to be a revolutionary.

# 4

# People of the Night

*Power was given to him that sat thereon to take
peace from the earth* (Rev. 6:4).

For relaxation and peace of mind I developed the
habit of taking long walks after dark. This night was perfect. The bright moon made walking easy. I stayed near
the trees, keeping in their shadows. The weather was
pleasant and the world was deceitfully peaceful. I sat down
under a tree on the bank of an old strip mine. From a
distance came the song of a whippoorwill and the bark of a
coon hound. It seemed impossible to think of the Tribulation.

I was leaning back against the trunk of a tree, eyes
closed and half asleep, drinking in the peace of the night.
Suddenly I was brought from dreamland by the sound of
low voices and footsteps. My military training caused me
instinctively to seek cover. In the shadow of the tree, flat
on the ground with grass and undergrowth around me, I
could easily be stepped on before being detected.

Before reaching me, the people turned toward the
right and descended into the old strip pit. As soon as I felt
it was safe, I attempted to follow them. But even with the

bright moonlight, they had vanished. Not a sound could be heard, and not a movement could be seen. Although I realized it could be dangerous, I was determined to find out more about these people. It was useless, however, to attempt to follow them in the dark.

The following day seemed long because I was eager to solve the previous night's mystery. As soon as it was dark I planned to go back to the strip pit. I did not mention to Matt and June what had occurred.

In order to blend into the night, I dressed in black; and as soon as I was away from our hideaway, I blackened my face with coal dust. But my efforts that night were fruitless. I neither saw nor heard anyone.

On the fourth night my search was rewarded. I had been in hiding only a few minutes when I heard voices, and could distinguish three people. I followed them but remained at a safe distance. Suddenly an undetermined noise caused me to freeze. It was one of those unaccountable things. You hear something but not distinctly. After a few minutes of waiting I decided that it was my imagination. Very cautiously I moved in the direction where I had last seen the people. As quietly as possible I felt my way along a deep gulley that led down into the strip mine. A movement caused me to whirl to my right, but I remember nothing else.

While regaining consciousness, my mind was still telling me there was danger to my right. I tried to move in that direction only to discover that my hands and feet were tied.

Gaining full consciousness, I was staring into a small fire. The flames cast dark dancing shadows upon the walls and ceiling of an old abandoned mine. Turning my head in spite of the pain, I saw that I was surrounded by men with covered faces.

My movements caused all eyes to turn toward me.

Then one of the men began asking questions in a voice that was calm but demanding: "Who are you?"

I did not answer. Was it fear, anger, or confusion? I am not sure.

The next question was icy. "Why don't you have the Mark of the Beast?"

Suddenly I saw hope. If these people were connected with the secret police of the World Peace Bureau, they would refer to the Economic Mark—not the "Mark of the Beast." There was only one thing to do—take the chance that they were friendly.

"I am Stephen Miles. There is no Mark of the Beast because I am a Christian."

The same icy voice cut in, "Who is your father?"

"Most people called him Jim."

A distant voice, with just a tinge of fear asked, "Why were you following our people with your face blackened?"

I quickly reported my experience of hearing voices and of my own fear of strangers in the area. I did not, however, refer to June and Matt or where we lived.

Just as I was hopeful that my answers had satisfied them, the leader lifted his hand. All the men reached down and lifted huge rocks. Again I was confronted by the stern voice of the leader.

"Stephen Miles, you have defied Prince Goldbar in refusing to take the Economic Mark. However, if we forge the Mark upon your hand for a price, will you accept it? If not, are you prepared to die?"

In the apple orchard of my father's home I had made my committment to Christ. If there had ever been any doubt in my mind concerning my willingness to die for Christ, it was erased. A strange calmness came over me.

"Men," I said, "I failed Christ many times. For the love of self, I sought worldly recognition when I should have taught God's word for His glory. I am helpless. I cannot defend myself. Do with me as you will, but I cannot deny Christ again."

The hooded men looked at each other, as they reached silent agreement. The leader removed his hood, and the others followed his action. I could not believe it. With his hood removed, I recognized my Uncle Tim.

"Uncle Tim, what is this? Man, you had me frightened almost to death. What's going on here?"

"It's quite simple, Steve. This is the meeting place of Tribulation Christians. You were following us to our service. You know that to be discovered is to die. Because of this we keep the meeting place secret and the entrance guarded."

Then with a smile he added, "By the way, your head had a sharp meeting with Ben's stick. Sorry, Steve, but we had to test you to be sure of your commitment."

Then a neighborhood boy of my childhood stepped forward with a self-conscious smile to cut the rope that bound me.

"Sorry, Steve, but you know we have to be careful. When you failed to give the signal on the trail, I did what the rules say to do. I stopped you."

This experience could have been a drama right out of the Early Church. Even as the Roman Empire had tried to exterminate the early Christian community, the Antichrist would seek to destroy the Tribulation Christians. To worship Christ meant to hide. To be discovered was to be forced to recant or die.

"Ben, you said something about giving the signal. What kind of a signal?" I asked.

Ben hesitated and looked toward my Uncle Tim. The look was a question that asked, "Can we trust him?" Uncle Tim nodded affirmatively.

"Steve," Ben answered, "it is the word that has expressed the hope of Christians of all ages. The signal is—"

I broke in before he completed his statement: "Ben, you mean the signal word is 'Eternal life?'"

"Yes," Ben replied, "when a person gets to the large rock on the right of the path, he must say 'Life,' or he will be stopped. At service time the entrance is always guarded by two of us."

Now I was seated with the others around the fire. It was cold in the old mine, and the warmth of the fire was welcomed. Uncle Tim, who had never been a Christian until after the Rapture, told me that the Christian band had formed following chance meetings at the cemetery. They had seen each other standing by the open graves of resurrected relatives. Without a word, they came to understand each other.

For many months after the Rapture they had met secretly in homes. But as world conditions became more serious, they found the homes too dangerous and had moved the meeting place to this old coal mine.

They agreed that I could stay for the meeting. Uncle Tim took charge. The first item of discussion was the Economic Mark or, as they called it, "the Mark of the Beast." One of the Christians had made a stencil with which they could simulate the mark.

Was it compromising to use this counterfeit mark? It meant death to appear in public places without the mark. And without it one could not buy food, clothing, or medicine. There seemed no way to survive without it.

The discussion went on for an hour. For some, to imitate the Mark was compromise but others saw this as the only way to survive the Tribulation. It was finally concluded that each person would have to make his own decision. My own mind was already made up. For me, there would be no compromise of any kind with the Mark of the Beast.

I assured the group that I would attend future meetings. No questions were asked about where I lived. I felt that Matt and June should be advised of this experience; and if they chose to do so, they could attend. I told Uncle Tim about them.

When I arrived home at the mine, I found an agitated couple.

"Where have you been? We have been worried to death!"

Within a few minutes I had told the whole story. For June, the idea of seeing and talking with other women was exciting. I suddenly realized that for almost four years she had talked with no one but Matt and me.

Sunday morning well before daylight we made our way toward the strip pit and the openings of the old coal mine.

"Steve," Matt said quietly, "think of all the times in the old days when we could have gone to church in the comfort of our cars, sat in the luxury of padded pews, and looked at the beauty of stained glass windows. But we went only often enough to keep up a religious front. When it cost us little, we gave little. Now it could cost us our lives to attend a worship service, and we are walking through the night to a coal mine."

"All Tribulation Christians are people of the night," I answered.

In a short time we pushed our way through the thick undergrowth that clustered in the gulley. As we approached the signal rock, I stepped ahead and announced softly but clearly, "Life." Out of the dark came the reply, "Eternal Life." I recognized Ben's voice. However, I said nothing more, and we moved ahead.

When we arrived at the mine, Matt immediately recognized Uncle Tim. June, Matt, and I were introduced. Several were present who had not been in the previous meeting including the entire Dobbs family: Mr. and Mrs.

Jerry Dobbs, their sons, James and Edward, and their daughter Cindy. In all, about 30 people were present. I recognized most of them. Like me, they had had Christian parents and had attended church; but they themselves had not accepted Christ. Now we were serving God in the years of the Beast.

The service was simple. We prayed, read the Bible, and Uncle Tim made a talk. We were advised to pray much because we must be strong enough to face death. I realized that this group had faced and accepted death as their portion. They had prepared themselves to die rather than recant if caught.

After the service I visited with Cindy Dobbs for a while. We had been in the first grade together. She had attended college at Wesley and had been a physical education teacher for several years. Cindy was one of those persons who radiates health and the joy of living—an attractive girl though a little on the chubby side.

Back at our mine home, June was her old self for the first time in almost four years.

She said: "Steve, I've found a wife for you, Cindy Dobbs. How romantic! Teacher, soldier, man of the world returns to his home town to marry his first-grade classmate."

During breakfast and through the day she chattered, laughed, and joked. It was wonderful to find a little sunshine in the world again. But the few light moments that we enjoyed never lasted long.

A speech by Prince Goldbar that night was the most vicious that he had made. For the first time he linked the Christians and Jews in his hate. His speech began with commendations of Hitler.

"Hitler lived ahead of his time. Furthermore, it was Hitler as a prophet who first recognized that the Jews were responsible for the legend of Jesus Christ as the Messiah.

63

It was the Jews who were responsible for Christianity and the Bible. It was the Jews who taught that there would be a Rapture. Knowing that Judeo-Christianity was the origin of the discontent in the world, Hitler and his followers paid a price with their lives to right the wrongs and bring peace to the earth. However, his work was cut short by his untimely death and his task was left unfinished.

"The death of Hitler was caused by the Christians. When they realized that the origin of Christianity was known, they knew well that they themselves would soon face their day of judgment. Out of this selfishness they plunged the whole world into war.

"Today I pledge to bring peace to the world. To do this, the Christians must be destroyed. I call upon all patriotic citizens of the world to stand up for what is right and good. Dedicate your lives to the cause of peace and goodwill. Be noble, brave, and strong. Rid the world of the cancer that has destroyed families and nations. Destroy Christians. They must be destroyed—on the streets, in the homes, on the jobs—wherever they are found.

"You are not just citizens, just police, soldiers, or government officers. You are the makers of a new world. In this new world there will be no 'thou shalt nots.' In our new world, no pleasure of any kind will be withheld. You are living at the rising of the sun. In this new day there will be no night, laughter will know no weeping, sweetness will have no bitterness.

"For this to be true, the Christians, those traitors against the human race, must be destroyed. The Jewish Founder of Christianity, Jesus Christ, taught sorrow and bloodshed. Please, dear citizens, do not blame me for this truth. Jesus taught violence without hesitation. I quote his very words, 'Think not that I am come to send peace on earth: I came not to send peace but a sword. For I am come to set a man at variance against his father, and a daughter against her mother, and a daughter in law against her mother in law.'[1] Now, I ask you, who brings trouble to the world and division to the family? I can tell you—the Christians.

"My fellow citizens, go back to the beginning of human history. Who started all of man's trouble? It was the Jew and his Bible. Man was in à garden, but God tried to withhold the best from him. It was my spirit that used a cooperative serpent to talk to Eve. I simply asked her if she would like to know the facts of good and evil. She did. Now tell me, what is wrong in seeking the truth, knowledge, and the facts of life? It was *not* wrong. It is simply that Deity tried to selfishly hold the truth to himself.

"So fearful did God become when He found out that I was leading men into truth that He immediately created strife. Instead of lifting man up, he placed a curse upon him and did all that He could to create permanent strife between man and the Prince of This World. I can prove this from the Bible. 'And I will put enmity between thee and the woman and between thy seed [the Prince of This World] and her seed [the one called Jesus]. It shall bruise thy head and thou shalt bruise his heel.'[2] This was a declaration of war that will not cease until every Jew and Christian is gone from the earth.

"Today, as the Prince of This World, I declare total war and complete extermination for every Jew and Christian in the world. Special peace troops have been organized for their extermination. This is not my choice as the Prince of This World, but it is a heavy duty placed upon me by the revolutionary groups called Christians and Jews.

---

1. Matt. 10:34-35.
2. Gen. 3:15.

"The Christians will not stand at attention when our flag is raised. They will not worship me, the Prince of This World, as God. Our police officers and our generals have been given orders. Jews and Christians must die. Soldiers must carry out the ideals of our world, the extermination of all enemies of the state.

"The world was not in turmoil when I first came to the earth. I was here before man came. The Intruder, Jesus, testified to this: 'I beheld Satan as lightning fall from heaven.'[3] I came in glory and power to withstand the Intruder, Jesus. The followers of Jesus have caused our chaotic conditions; they must be completely destroyed, or they will destroy us. The death of all Christians and Jews must be a united effort by a world organized for their complete extermination.

"Every reversal that we have experienced has been caused by the Christians and Jews—the world food shortage, the lack of complete cooperation, and the attack upon me. Therefore, without fear, every citizen must be engaged in the holy ritual of killing them. The glory, the pride, and the hope of our world goverment depend upon the death of these traitors.

"Christians and the Jews collectively are the enemy. They must answer for every death, sorrow, and tragedy that any man has ever known in the history of the world. It was the God of the Christians who passed the sentence of death and the curse of suffering upon man.

"As Prince of This World I have never willed the death of any man or woman. I am the lover of peace, the patron of happiness, and I have only one wish for all men—life, abundant joy, and pleasure now. I bid you good night, and the blessing of the Prince of This World."

There was nothing new in the speech. It was the same

---

3. Luke 10:18.

old harangue with added hate. We did not discuss it. There was really nothing we could say.

The hiding Christians had called a special meeting for Monday night. We decided that I alone would attend the conference. Most of the men from the Sunday service were there. Uncle Tim opened the meeting with prayer. He then quickly but calmly came to the point.

"Friends in Christ, many of us have been thinking, praying, and discussing the problems of the Mark of the Beast. Taking the mark is out for me. I feel it would be an act of betrayal. But going into our world without it is too dangerous. In his speech last night Goldbar again announced the death sentence on Christians. It seems to me that we have only two possible alternatives: We can continue to counterfeit the mark, which is the old situational ethics, or we must go into permanent hiding."

I felt sure that we were in for a long session. Back in the university such a proposition would have occasioned discussion for a week. How different things are when it is to do or die.

As a body, the Christians gave their answer. Mr. Jerry Dobbs was the spokesman.

"Tim, I've been thinking this over. Even to counterfeit the mark is to take the mark of Satan. I can't play the role of being the devil's servant. I cannot and will not do it any longer. We choose to go into permanent hiding. My family has everything packed and we are ready to move tomorrow night."

After the meeting, I talked with Mr. Dobbs and offered to catch our horses to help them move. He had two, but the more horses, the faster the moving could be done. It was agreed that I would come to his house just before midnight.

It was easy to catch two of our horses. Mr. Dobbs's farm bordered the pastureland leading to the strip pit area so there was no problem in arriving undetected at his house. But one's instincts take over at such a time. I stopped under a grove of oak trees a few hundred yards from his house. I watched, listened, and waited for any signs of activity. There were none. This was good. A normal household at midnight should be quiet and asleep.

I left the horses in the cover of the trees and went to the back door. Knocking softly, I said, "Life is good." It brought an immediate response. Mr. Dobbs was eager to get moved, and a pile of bundles was ready to be tied on the horses. He told me that James and Edward already had two horses loaded at the side of the house. Cindy came to the door and said she would go with me for my horses.

The next few minutes made this a night of terror. We had reached the horses and were prepared to start toward the house when Cindy cried, "Steve, look!"

We saw the headlights of cars coming at high speed. Red lights were flashing. Three cars skidded to a stop in front of, and to the side of the house. We had been betrayed. We did not know it at the time, but this was our first meeting with Prince Goldbar's Peace Troops.

Cindy started to run toward the house, but I knew that everything depended on hiding. I clamped my hand over her mouth and fell to the ground, pulling her with me. We rolled under a large fig tree with limbs that reached to the ground.

"Cindy," I whispered, "are you all right?"

I lifted my hand just enough for an answer. Her controlled whisper assured me that she was not hysterical. But what we saw and heard in the next few moments staggered the mind and emotions even of a war veteran.

The three cars quickly emptied. Chief of Police Jackson McKifer was in charge. In elementary school we had called him "Pug" McKifer, the bully. Big, red-faced, loud and vulgar, he had always tried to boss and dominate

68

every activity around him. With his new power under the world government of the Beast, "Pug" had come into his own. He was more than a local police chief; He had been appointed head of the Peace Troops in our area.

The family was soon lined up outside of the house. Now we knew the traitor. From the back seat of one of the cars stepped Alex Williams. I had known him as the proprietor of a general store.

"Chief McKifer," Williams's high-pitched voice croaked out. "I am prepared to testify that these people are Christians. They do not have the Economic Mark."

It was only then I realized that Cindy was whispering. "Steve, he's our neighbor. He's been spying on us. Why would he do this? I've known him all my life."

There was no time to explain that Williams was selling the lives of the Dobbs family in hopes of gaining special privileges and money from the world government.

I knew that I had to get Cindy away, and was whispering instructions to her when I heard McKifer say, "Alex, we've got four of them, but where's the girl?"

There was hope in his answer. "Chief, she's been away teaching for years. In fact, she's been home only occasionally." Williams spoke with pride in his position as an informer.

The events of the next few minutes were so ghastly that I could have easily fancied it was a nightmare. From the side of the house out of the darkness came the sound of gunfire. Almost simultaneously there was a terrifying scream or wail—how can I describe it? I saw one of Dobbs's horses race by. He had been shot. The unearthly, siren-like wails were still rising and falling from the wounded animal as it disappeared.

I had fought in Viet Nam, and had heard men die. But never had my nerves been shattered as they were by the

69

dying agony of this horse as he went crashing into the night.

Hot and wet with the perspiration of fear, I stared through dilated eyes toward the house, illuminated by the headlights of the cars. McKifer and his men opened fire on the Dobbs family. Holding hands, the four slumped to the ground. There was no mercy tonight. The followers of the Beast were in full control.

I was sobered to hear myself pray, "O God, have mercy." Mercy, however, was gone. This was the Tribulation.

There had been no sound from Cindy, but I could feel her tremble. Holding her hand with the hope that my presence would give some support, I whispered, "Follow me but stay down."

There was so much activity at the house I felt sure we could crawl away undetected. Leaving the horses tied, we crawled through the heavy brush, slowly and cautiously, every sense alert. We soon covered the short distance to the protection of the barn. Its black depths was like finding the comforting arms of a friend. From the cover of the barn, we were able to reach our escape route, a deep ditch.

After what seemed an eternity, I felt free to speak to Cindy. "I'm sorry. I know it sounds weak and inadequate, but Matt, June, and I will help you all we can."

As if she had not heard me, she said, "Steve, they were so brave. I watched them. They didn't beg for their lives. It was almost as if they saw someone in heaven. They were calm and unafraid. Steve, I believe they saw Jesus as they died. They are with Him now. Thank God. They were brave. They were not intimidated by McKifer and his men. My family were the conquerors. Steve, do you remember what the Bible said about the Tribulation Christians?"

70

"Yes, Cindy, I remember. 'And they overcame him by the blood of the Lamb, and by the word of their testimony; and they loved not their lives unto the death' (Rev. 12:11)."

For an hour Cindy and I stumbled and splashed our way into the night. Again the haunting thought came back to me, We are people of the dark. Like hunted animals Christians must move by night and live underground by day.

When we reached an area of safety we looked back. In the direction of the Dobbs' home the heavens were red with the glow of fire. McKifer's destruction was thorough. However, one may be sure that he and his men had taken everything of value before they burned the buildings. Having killed and tasted of the spoil, McKifer and men like him all over the world would kill again and again.

Wet and disheveled, Cindy followed me by a circuitous route to the mine. We moved quickly to the door. It had been so carefully camouflaged that one could walk by in the thick undergrowth and never see it. Pressing my face close to the door, I called softly, "Matt, June." Immediately the door was opened.

After one look at Cindy, without waiting for an explanation June took over. It was about an hour before June came out of her room. She reported that Cindy had bathed, her cuts and scratches had been treated, and she was sleeping the rest of the exhausted. In as few words as possible I told of our night of horror.

Cindy rested all day, but in the evening joined the rest of us for dinner. An extra person was no problem. In preparing for the Tribulation we had prepared for emergencies. There was enough food, oil for cooking and heating, clothing, and medicine for years.

During the dinner we reflected on the experience at the Dobbs home. For the first time we began to question

71

the wisdom of our living so close to town. True, we were a few miles distant, and well hidden from the nearest house, but was this enough?

After eating, we gathered for the news. The program was typical in that the major part was filled with declarations of the glories of the Prince of This World. The item of special interest was an announcement that the Prince would speak immediately following the news.

Bishop Costo presented the Prince, who first reviewed the programs under his administration. His appearance was again kind and thoughtful as he discussed his theme of world prosperity and peace.

But suddenly his whole countenance changed. His face looked distorted and menacing as he turned on the Christians and Jews, seeking to prove his rightful place as ruler of the world. He raved more than an hour, declaring that He was the Messiah and the only savior. Repeatedly he used the Bible to prove his identity.

"Even the murderous Christians and their so-called Holy Bible confess to my being the rightful ruler of the world. They refer to me as 'the prince of this world,'[4] 'the prince of the power of the air,'[5] 'an angel of light,'[6] and 'the god of this world.'[7] The Book of the Christians speaks plainly of my position but they will not recognize the authority of their own Book. They have a death feud with the Alliance of the World.

"I seek only good, pleasure, peace, and prosperity. The reactionary Christians seek hate, pain, war, and destruction. They killed me, but I was resurrected. They seek to sabotage this government in every part of the world.

---

4. John 14:30.
5. Eph. 2:2.
6. 2 Cor. 11:14.
7. 2 Cor. 4:4.

72

"In Israel two henchmen have been speaking against me day and night. They refer to themselves as the 'two witnesses.' This is treason. For weeks some of my best advisors have been negotiating with Israel. No nation on earth has gained more from my administration. Their Temple has been rebuilt, their cities and lands developed. It has been my power that has forced peace upon all the Arab nations so the Jews could rebuild their Temple. Still there is rebellion and hate in the heart of Israel against me.

"It is with deep regret that for the first time I have ordered the army to move against a nation. The armed forces of the Alliance are now in charge in Jerusalem. A major part of the army of Israel is in hiding at Petra.

"I am speaking to you from the Temple at Jerusalem. It is for the welfare of all men that I make the following proclamation. The men who called themselves the two witnesses have been executed. Their bodies are lying in the street as a warning to Jews and Christians. It must be clearly understood that all who dwell in the world must worship me. Anyone without the patriotic Economic Mark is sentenced to death. All citizens have the authority to kill any enemy of the state who has not accepted the Mark. The Senate has voted a $1,000 reward for the apprehension, dead or alive, of any enemy of the Alliance of the World. It is understood by this government that anyone without the Economic Mark is classified as a Christian and, therefore, is worthy of death. If their Messiah can protect them, let Him do so. If I am not stronger than their Jesus, let them worship Him. If I am stronger than He, they must worship me. Christians are to be put to death. All must choose today whom they will serve.

"Times have changed. If our good world with its good life is to continue, it must be protected from the hate of the Christians. Suffering and death has always been a major mood of Christianity. If people will look at the facts of history, any honest man or woman will agree with me. From the time of Jesus to the present, Christianity has brought division and death. Christ split the Jewish nation. Christianity itself has been divided between the Protestants and Roman Catholics. These same Christians would tear our utopia to pieces.

"Following this program the government will explain the steps that are being taken to protect you from the Christians.

"Goodnight, and may the peace and joy of the Prince of This World be with you; may the pleasures of the Alliance of the World abide forever."

Bishop Casto appeared immediately. Without introduction he began:

"For those who doubt the treacherous purposes of the Christians, this program will give you some insight into their underground revolutionary efforts. We will begin in Israel. The first picture is of the two ministers who preached treason."

The cameras focused on two bloody bodies lying in the street. People passed. Some looked. A few stopped, but the majority simply walked on.

"The next two pictures," stated Bishop Costo, "are of Christians in the United States who are guilty of revolutionary activity by refusing to accept the Economic Mark. By this action they are guilty of trying to undermine the economic stability of the Alliance of the World."

A group of 20 people appeared on the screen. A police captain came forward to make them expose their hands. There was no Mark.

The officer spoke to a boy who appeared to be about 18.

"What is your name?"

"Sir, my name is Fred Howell."

74

"What are you doing here?" demanded the officer.

"I was reared in the church. I knew that I should be a Christian, but I was influenced by the unbelievers and left Christ out of my life. However, when the Christians were raptured away, I . . ."

He did not complete his statement. The policeman slapped the boy in the face and ordered him to cease his revolutionary talk.

Now the picture was enlarged to reveal a ring of policemen around the Christians. An elderly man and woman supported each other. A young couple stood arm in arm. Some of the group huddled together as if they were a family. Their facial expressions led one to believe that they knew what was coming next.

The Christians were lined up. Policemen raised their rifles and at a signal opened fire. The Christians fell to the ground. Their bodies were loaded on a truck and taken away.

The next picture was from London. A band of 10 Christians were locked in a room. One could clearly see the gas vapors as they filled the death chamber. From the movement of their lips it was evident that they were singing.

In city after city the pictures were the same—bands of Christians standing together, dying together, and being buried together. For one hour the documentary film from all around the world continued. The Prince had intensified his war on the Christians. Drunk with power, he had challenged men and God.

After the last scene, Bishop Costo emphasized that if a citizen knew the location of a Christian and did not report it immediately, he himself was a traitor and would be executed. At the same time he repeated the offer of $1,000 for each Christian who was reported.

We were all shaken. One cannot be indifferent to

living under a sentence of death and being reminded that the person who reports you will be rewarded. We realized anew that we were people of the night and of the underground. How foolishly we had lived. Refusing to believe in the Rapture and great Tribulation, we had drunk deep from the cup of pleasure only to find death written at the bottom of the cup.

Sunday again found shadowy figures moving through the predawn. Fearful people with dilated eyes trying to penetrate the darkness. Groping hands reached out to find the way. With furtive looks, listening, fearful of being followed, they moved toward their meeting place. It was with deep sighs of relief that they approached the signal rock to whisper, "Life" and to hear the welcomed reply, "Eternal life."

This Sunday morning Uncle Tim read the Sermon on the Mount. After the reading and a few comments, prayers were offered by three of the men. Their major plea was for courage to face what lay ahead.

As soon as the service ended, Uncle Tim gave a speech that made me realize there was a Christian underground.

"Before we leave there is some important news that I have for all of you. First, we must double our caution. "Pug" McKifer has received recognition from Washington and from the Alliance of the World for his vigilance in destroying Christian bands. Word has come that he is training dogs for hunting Christians. We must be on guard every moment. McKifer is ruthless. He'll be more so now that there's a reward for each Christian, dead or alive.

"It is recommended by the Christian underground that each one should keep his home a secret. If one of us should be captured and tortured he could reveal the homes of others. It is also suggested that we make frequent changes of our meeting place. We'll come to the signal rock next Sunday. Here each one will give the code word

'Life.' A new signal will be given the group at each service, and the meeting place for the next gathering will be announced.

"It's also been suggested that one of our members be selected as a coordinator. This person will be the only one in our group who'll know where each one lives. He'll also know the supplies that are stored in each home. We'll share and help one another."

Andrew Green spoke. "I nominate Tim Chandler as coordinator." Immediately there was a united voice vote of approval.

"I accept the vote," Uncle Tim responded. "I do know every foot of the county, and I have a contact with the underground. After the meeting I would like for a member of each family to give me information on where you live and what supplies you have."

To my complete surprise, Uncle Tim further announced, "I'm appointing Steve Miles as my assistant in charge of supplies. It's important that the needs of all our people be met. Winter will soon be here, and we must all try to stay well. But where there is illness, treatment must be given at once.

"For the time being," Uncle Tim continued, "I'll set up my headquarters here in this mine. I'm asking Ben and Rob to stay with me as helpers."

Each family met with Uncle Tim, giving directions to their homes and listing their supplies. When I met with him, he asked me to return that night.

One by one the families vanished into the blackness. Again the haunting thought came back, "We are people of the night." This thought was becoming an obsession with me.

Matt and June led the way; Cindy and I followed as we made our way back to our cave-home. After the walk in the cool morning we were all ready for a good breakfast. Eggs preserved in a barrel of salt water, and salted meat were soon cooking over the flame of our oil stove. Three years of preparation had paid off with an abundance of food.

The talk during breakfast was serious. We agreed that none of us should go out during the day and that we should be careful not to make a path toward our door. Then the question came up about McKifer's dogs. What could be done if hounds were on our trail?

Unfortunately, none of us knew very much about dogs. Matt had heard that vinegar, if it were placed in each footstep, would cause them to lose the trail. But June had heard that pepper was best. Cindy had been told that the best thing was to find water and walk in it long enough for the dogs to lose the scent. We agreed that we would try one or all of these if it were ever necessary. It would be simple to take a can of pepper on each trip. One thing was sure—none of us would ever return to the mine with dogs after us.

It was cold and dark when I started out to keep my appointment with Uncle Tim. I had learned to move quickly in the darkness, and in a short time I was approaching the signal rock. As I arrived it was routine to say "I enjoy life." The response came back, "Eternal life is good." As I moved past the big rock, I said to the two concealed guards, "You fellows are going to need protection before the cold winter rains begin."

"We've got it," Ben answered. Then I discovered where Ben stood, protected by a rock that projected out over him like an umbrella.

When I arrived at the mine, Uncle Tim was sitting by a small fire. Living in a coal mine, there was no shortage of fuel.

Uncle Tim quickly got to the point.

"Steve, I've chosen you to be my helper, but you may

feel free to refuse when I tell you your assignment. It's our duty to watch over these people. At times they'll be unwise and hard to reason with. Even if they act like children, we must protect them from their own foolishness and from the Beast.

"Here are listed all our resources under the name of each family. It won't be wise to keep any of this in writing. Study the list. Memorize what you can. Your memory will be the only inventory used to supply the needs of the people. The list must be destroyed.

"Now for the most serious part of our meeting. Many evenings about one hour after dark a bottle is dropped into the creek at Ray's Crossing. I don't know who does this. All I know is that there is a Christian underground. I don't know the extent or who heads this movement. Before I went into hiding, a letter was left at my house advising me that I could receive news if I'd check for a bottle that would be thrown from Ray's Bridge into the creek. I've never tried to find out who throws the bottle, but one has been delivered each time there's any major move by the Beast."

"Sure thing, Uncle Tim," I spoke lightly but inwardly I felt uneasy. "I'll memorize the inventory records and then destroy them. I'll check for the bottle each day. When any news comes, I'll report to you immediately."

I started back to the mine in a cold rain. The damp coldness seemed to reach with icy fingers to my very bones. Maybe I was still shaken by the Dobbs experience— hearing the screams of a wounded horse, and seeing a family shot down—or maybe I was tired. But I could not help wondering, What is the use? How can a few people hiding underground and moving by night hold out against the whole world? Did not the Bible admit that all who dwell upon the earth would worship the Beast? How does one serve Christ in a world where it is dangerous to even know a Christian?

It was with relief of body and spirit that I arrived at home. Cindy had cooked a dinner that would have lifted the spirit of any man. Hot food to eat and coffee to drink soon conquered the chill that had tormented my body.

Dinner had been over for about an hour when Uncle Tim came. He was our first visitor. Matt and June greeted him with enthusiasm.

"Come in, Uncle Tim. There's plenty of dinner left over. Sit down for a hot dinner and some coffee."

"No, thanks, June. There isn't time. While Andrew Green was cutting wood, he injured his foot. It's a bad cut. Cindy, I believe that in physical education you were trained in first aid?"

"Yes, I was, and I'm willing to go and do all I can."

"Steve," Uncle Tim spoke softly like a tired man, "You had better come with us. It may be a long, hard trip."

Within a few minutes Cindy had selected first aid supplies for the treatment of a cut. Uncle Tim led the way into the night. Again the obsessive thought came to me, "We are people whose companion is fear, whose dwelling is a coal mine. We are not only people of the night, but we live in the shadowy world of the underground."

It seemed we had walked for miles when we finally came to an old muddy road used at one time for hauling coal. Turning left we followed the road across the creek into the hills. At times the climb was steep. I could not help but ask,

"Uncle Tim, don't you think that we should stop and rest?"

His answer was the voice of an exhausted man, "Steve, there's a hurt man and a worried family waiting for us."

It seemed to me that we had been climbing for an hour when Uncle Tim said abruptly, "We're here."

Standing by a thick grove of pine trees, Uncle Tim called softly, "This is a good life."

The answer came back, "Life is needed." Almost immediately Mrs. Green stepped from behind a holly tree that grew among the pines. "This way," she whispered. She pulled open a wood-framed door that was camouflaged with tree limbs. They also had been fortunate in finding a dry mine in which to live.

Mrs. Green had boiled water, and bathed the deep ax cut in the right foot of her husband. Even so, the foot was red and Mr. Green had a fever. Cindy examined the cut and filled the wound with sulfa powder. The patient was given aspirin. When he was asleep, we assured Mrs. Green that we would return the next night.

The ground was damp from a soft rain, and the moon played hide-and-seek with the clouds. It was a cold, wet night. We were near Black Creek, and I was thinking of all the times that I had hunted coons at night in this area.

"Boy," I exclaimed softly. "What a good night for the dogs to run."

Cindy's answer was not in response to my statement. "Steve, listen." Those were the urgent words of a brave but frightened girl.

What I heard was at one time a thrill, but tonight it was terrifying. From the distance came the deep, long bay of hounds on a chase. The more I listened, the more uneasy I felt. We all knew that this could be some boys hunting game, or it could be McKifer hunting Christians at $1,000 per person. If this were McKifer, and if we were caught, Uncle Tim and I would be shot. But the degrading treatment of Cindy would be more horrible than death. Uncle Tim lost no time in choosing our course of action.

"We must assume that this is McKifer. The dampness

will make it easy for the dogs to follow us. If they stay on our trail, they'll go directly to the Greens' hideaway. We must prevent this. Steve, you and Cindy go to the right, away from the dogs but toward the creek. If this is McKifer and his gang, I'll get close enough to distract the dogs and have them follow me into the woods away from the Greens'."

I interrupted with, "Uncle Tim, but . . ."

I got no farther. "No time to talk, Steve. Get moving!" Hand in hand, Cindy and I ran through the woods.

Fortunately, the three years of work on the farm had kept me in top physical condition. Cindy's activities as a physical education teacher had kept her muscles firm, but it seemed a long time before we reached the creek. We both knew what we had to do. Without hesitation we waded into the icy water.

Our fear and excitement kept us from feeling the full effects of the cold. We moved as rapidly and as quietly as possible upstream. At the same time we were hoping and praying that any dogs that may have picked up our trail would find some scent on the bank or in the water that would lead them downstream. To throw the dogs off, I dropped my handkerchief into the water hoping that they would scent it and follow as it floated downstream. We walked in the creek for about a mile, then climbed out on the side opposite from our mine. In spite of the cold we moved so fast that there was a minimum of discomfort.

After we had walked about another mile on the bank of the creek, we turned and retraced our steps for half the distance. We could no longer hear the hounds and could only wonder what had happened to Uncle Tim.

We had come to a place where the creek was narrow, and to our happy surprise there were tall trees covered with vines growing on the bank. Boyhood experience came to the rescue. Within a few minutes I had selected a vine that grew to a tall tree with limbs reaching over the creek. I tested the vine for strength. Determining that it was strong, I cut it loose at the bottom, intending to use it as a swing.

"Cindy," I said, "stay here while I test it to see if we can swing across the creek."

With a good running start I had no problem swinging to the other side. In a moment I was back. Since Cindy had been reared in this area she needed no explanation. Taking the vine from me, she was across and calling for me to catch the vine as she swung it back. Within a moment I, too, was across and we were on our way.

In spite of the cold and rain, there was a thrill holding to each other as we raced through the night. We even laughed once when we tried to imagine our appearance, soaked and muddy from the trip up the creek. But our joy was sobered by our fears for Uncle Tim. Where was he? Where were the dogs? How could we cope with McKifer and his men?

It was late when we reached our mine. June had anticipated that we would be cold, wet, and hungry, so within a few minutes we were comfortable from hot baths, the warm fire, and hot food and drink.

Our problem still centered on McKifer, his dogs, and what had happened to Uncle Tim. We all feared that he was hurt or dead, but we were unwilling to admit this even to ourselves. Where was Uncle Tim? I was preparing to go looking for him when we were electrified by a soft call out of the darkness, "Life is good in the dark and rain." Immediately we were at the door.

Uncle Tim was fatigued, wet, and dirty, but there was a twinkle in his eyes and laughter on his lips. Wrapped in warm blankets and drinking hot coffee he told us his experiences.

"You and Cindy had a head start of about 10 minutes

before I saw the dogs. They were hard on the trail leading to the Greens' home. According to our plan, I dropped my handkerchief in the road and ran into the woods. The dogs came after me, and they were followed by three men. I couldn't see them clearly, but I'm sure it was McKifer and two of his men.

"When the dogs came after me," Uncle Tim continued, "I ran into the best luck of my life. I found myself in a herd of cattle. When I jumped on the back of a large cow, she took off like a bullet. Most of the frightened cattle stampeded. This gave me cover. A few of the cows turned to defend their calves and attacked the dogs. The best that I could see, the dogs ran. Anyway, I was free and didn't hear the dogs again. I'm sure that McKifer and his men never saw me, and I'm just as sure that they're completely puzzled about what happened to sidetrack their dogs. But they'll be back."

In spite of the lighter side of the experience trying to envision Uncle Tim riding a cow, in our hearts we thanked God for His wonderful deliverance. But we all knew that we would be facing danger from the dogs again.

The following Sunday just before day, moving through the predawn like illegal shadows, we Christians headed for our meeting place. There Uncle Tim spoke to us of the suffering of Christ. As His servants we, too, would suffer. The difference was that Christ did no evil. We, on the other hand, had done wrong. We deserved all the fear and suffering that came to us.

After the service, Uncle Tim called a business meeting. On the previous day I had brought him a message from Ray's Crossing. This was his concern. Word of the danger of the dogs had spread through the Christian underground. A recommendation had been sent out that if pursued, ground hot pepper be placed in one's footsteps. Also, if possible, the dogs should be killed. It was reported that they had led to the capture of five Christians. They had also trapped, attacked, and killed two women.

From the discussion it seemed that the pepper would be so irritating to the nostrils of the dogs that they would be unable to resume trailing for days. The idea was a good one, but it became evident that pepper was in short supply. The Christians had moved from their homes to the mines so hurriedly that pepper held a low priority. There was only one thing to do. The dogs must be killed.

Mr. Green recommended that getting rid of the dogs should be left to Uncle Tim, Ben, Rob, and me. Ben and Rob were our woodsmen. Ben was casual when he asked if there were any rat poison. It was in good supply because the Christians in the community had known that moving into an old mine would involve a battle with rats.

Ben and Rob explained their plan. They would trap a rabbit, cut it into bite-sized pieces and put enough poison in each piece to kill a dog. Ben, Rob, and I were to carry out the rest of the plan.

The next day we prepared our bait. We knew that McKifer usually started his hunt as soon as it was dark. It was also well known that McKifer began his hunt at Ray's Crossing when he came to our area. Our plan was to go to Ray's Crossing and walk back into the woods. As soon as the dogs were on our trail, we would begin dropping the poisoned meat.

McKifer came the first night with two men and six dogs, three bloodhounds and three German shepherds. Immediately they were on our trail. The plan was perfect, and with a quarter of a mile start we felt secure. Jogging deeper into the woods, we dropped the poisoned meat as we ran. The baying of the hounds rolling off the hills as they closed in seemed to be no real threat.

However, it was not long until we knew that something was wrong. The dogs were getting menacingly close.

Suddenly I knew. I should have known from the beginning. In the military our dogs had been trained never to take meat on the trail.

"Ben, Rob," I shouted, "we must get away from those dogs!" We had brought some of our precious hot pepper for just such an emergency. We quickly sprinkled it on our tracks and moved to the creek, where we waded for a mile. We were free.

According to a previous agreement we reported to Uncle Tim. Ben told of our plan and its failure. I explained our error in forgetting that trained dogs will not eat on the trail. I suggested, however, that they would probably eat the poisoned meat in their pens. Uncle Tim shook his head.

"For any of us to go into town or to go near the jail to feed the dogs would be playing with death. Even trying to slip in at night would be too much of a risk. We must find some other way."

We parted with the understanding that we would meet the next night. This would be Friday, but as it turned out, this was too late to save Matt, June, Cindy, and me from an experience of terror.

Thursday night we four decided that we would take a predawn trip to see the Greens. Mr. Green had been suffering a recurring problem with his foot. Cindy felt that he was not giving it proper rest.

Friday morning was cold and we bundled up in heavy clothing, but had an easy trip. After examining and treating Mr. Green, we all enjoyed eating. Following breakfast we had prayer, and started home in the predawn. There was no worry about McKifer because we had never encountered him in a predawn raid.

We were still some distance from Ray's Crossing when we were brought to full alertness. Far away in the darkness we heard the sound that had haunted us in our dreams—the sound of dogs on the trail. They were in swift pursuit, hot on the trail that we had made earlier going to the Greens.

Our supply of pepper was exhausted. We had covered the trail from our home and also the path to the home of the Greens. Both were saved, but we were caught between them. The dogs were a mile or more away but coming toward us from the creek. There was only one thing to do: we had to run.

There was no time to devise a careful plan of escape. We had to run and think at the same time. We were four unarmed and hard beset Christians—Matt and June, Cindy, and I. We ran in the darkness so black that six feet was enough to blanket one into complete invisibility. It was a darkness of silence save for our running and the distant baying of the hounds.

In such darkness one's imagination could see better than one's eyes. My imagination was torturing as I saw the eyes of the dogs blazing, nostrils wide, and mouths foaming. The thought of June and Cindy being torn by these killers was maddening.

We continued to run as fast as the irregular ground and black night would permit. Trees and undergrowth struck out at our faces, scraping, chafing, and fighting us for every inch of progress. It was hard to fight off the conviction that further effort to escape the hounds of McKifer was hopeless. Whatever we did there was that endless baying, that long drawn-out howling demand for our lives from behind us—and getting closer.

Dawn found us blood-smeared, limping on blistered feet, and Matt with a sore neck. While running in the darkness, a low limb had caught him under the chin flipping him into the air and on his back.

With pounding hearts and heaving lungs, we pushed on. The only factor guiding our direction had been the desire to get away from the dogs. We still had no plan for escape. In anger I slapped my face to try to clear my mind. It seemed that I had been running all my life. Now in the first dawn I could see that we were approaching the edge of the woods. In spite of the deep, booming bark of the dogs we stopped at the edge of the woods to survey the clearing. We all stared in utter disbelief. Running in the darkness we had circled around to the back of my father's home. The clearing was where my father had planted his crop for years.

There was no time for reminiscing. The sound of the dogs crashing through the undergrowth was dangerously close.

"Run, run!" I called. I had an idea. There was hope. I remembered a lumber mill between the old home and town. On a siding the railroad workers usually kept a pump car. Cindy and June had been brave but it was obvious they were near the end of their endurance. We were at least a quarter of a mile from the mill, but they kept running. How I prayed for the handcar to be there.

"There it is!" I cried.

"And here come the dogs" yelled Matt.

Snarling, red-eyed, and with foam-covered mouths, the killers were upon us. I struggled with all my strength to get the handcar on the rails. Matt, June, and Cindy had picked up clubs and began to fight off the dogs.

I heard the howl of a wounded animal, and then felt the impact of a body. In a flying leap one of the dogs had knocked me down, but Matt sent the dog flying with a blow of his club. In another minute that seemed like a century, the car was on the rails, and we were on the car. Cindy and I pumped while Matt and June fought off the dogs. Matt had knocked out two of the German shepherds. The others stood snarling, but at a safe distance from the clubs, as the car began to move.

Cindy and I pumped the car while June and Matt stood ready for an attack. But the dogs had had enough. Evidently Matt had wounded their leader, and they made no effort to pursue us. In five minutes we had passed the railroad station and moved on toward Black Creek.

"We're out of sight of the dogs," June gasped.

I replied, "As we pass over Black Creek, we must drop into the water. We'll have several miles to wade, but this is the only way we can be sure the dogs will not pick up our trail."

My suggestion was accepted. We were too tired for talk. Utterly fatigued, we splashed up the creek and walked home in silence.

# 5

# Wounded

*Power was given . . . that they should kill one another*
(Rev. 6:4).

On Monday Matt, Ben, Rob, and I met with Uncle
Tim. Something had to be done immediately about the
dogs. Word had come through the bottle drop that
McKifer was adding three Russian wolf hounds. We would
never have escaped if these had been in the pack during
our recent experience.

Uncle Tim's idea was to electrocute the dogs. There
would be an element of danger but not as much as the
earlier idea of trying to slip into town to poison them.

We would set a trap, let the dogs come to us, and
electrocute them. At Ray's Crossing we would begin a trail
for the dogs to follow which would lead them to a shallow
pond of water. The trail would have to be long enough for
the dogs to outdistance the men and, therefore, be out of
sight of McKifer and his crew. The pond must have a tree
in the center and be near an electric line. Ben would have
no trouble splicing a connection into a live wire.

We agreed that this was the right idea. We would meet
Tuesday morning two hours before daylight to set the trap.

Before then we would all try to find materials and select the best location.

I decided to go back to my old home for the wire. It was dawn when I arrived at the farm. I had come in the back way through the woods and stood facing an open field between the barn and me. I paused to evaluate the situation, because to be seen could mean death.

Everything was quiet. The house and barn looked as they had for years except for the high grass and weeds. I moved to step into the clearing, but intuitively I stopped. My senses were alert from the instinctive desire for survival. I saw nothing unusual, but moved back into the woods and to a new vantage point. Again I visually searched the house, barn, and grounds. Again I saw nothing.

Even though I was on a mission to save the lives of all the Christians in our area, I did not feel brave or heroic. The obsessive thought came again: "We are people of the night." How strange to fear the light and open places! It was against man's very nature.

The fear of being seen was enough to keep my eyes roving, set my heart pounding, and tense every muscle. I was no coward. I had fought in Viet Nam, and was decorated for bravery. But how few of us against the world! I feared torture. I was afraid of being torn and dragged to my death by dogs. I desired to hold on to life.

I moved back into the woods and followed an old cow trail north. I halted again and again as I skirted the edge of the forest. It was no more than a quarter of a mile across the naked pastureland to the barn. But the thought of the bark of a dog, the sound of a gun, or the lurking eyes of McKifer made stepping into the open pasture sickening.

Fear makes a person more alive, sensitive, and aware. I was very conscious of the early dawn, of the freshness of the air, of the birds and the animal life. I drank in the beauty of the day and the exhilaration of nature. But in spite of the coolness, perspiration burned my eyes and stained my shirt. I felt a strong urge to pull away from the pasture and the house. I shrank from exposure.

How strange that my home of a lifetime should now hold such a threat for me. I licked my dry lips, took a deep breath, moved close to a wire fence that stretched to the barn and stepped into the clearing. My ears recorded the pounding of my heart as I listened for the bark of the dogs. I felt defenseless and found myself foolishly seeking the protection of the fence.

It may have been the movement of the barn door. Either something moved or I heard a noise. Again my military training of acting instinctively came to my rescue. I dropped into the tall grass by the fence. In my shelter I was almost invisible. From there I watched the door of the barn with no fear of being seen. The minutes dragged.

Did I hear or see anything? Was it just my nerves? Still I waited. A fly buzzed around my face. The sun was becoming warm. A rabbit hopped by. Still I waited. My thoughts drifted to Cindy and a desire to have known her in better days and under different circumstances.

Suddenly the doors of the barn opened. There stood Alex Williams. He had backed his truck into the barn and had helped himself to all that he wanted. He was stealing hay, corn, and feed supplies that he could sell. With a sigh of relief I watched him drive away.

With Williams out of sight, I still waited and watched for further movement. There was none. I ran quickly to the barn. Within minutes I had collected the wire and was ready to return to the woods. As warily as any pioneer scout in Indian country I stood at the door of the barn with every sense alert. I looked, listened, and felt the atmosphere. There was no movement or sound.

Quickly I covered the distance from the barn to the woods. With an elated spirit and light heart I headed home. Mission accomplished! The trees looked friendly and close. In their shade I felt protected and safe.

With little effort I glided noiselessly down the cow trail, but this relaxation almost destroyed me. Thoughts of Cindy, Matt, and June filled my mind. This preoccupation caused me to walk practically into the arms of Sheriff McKifer as I reached the clearing near Black Creek.

"Hello, Christian," he called. Without answering, I acted. With the wire in my left hand, my right fist shot out with my full weight behind it. I heard a savage cry of anger and I saw his gun fall as McKifer tumbled into the creek. Simultaneously, I heard the explosion as his gun struck the ground, and I felt the impact of a bullet hitting my right hand.

Then I ran—over rocks, through bushes, along cow trails, toward the creek bank. I knew well enough that McKifer was not alone. Looking back I got a glimpse of men on the hills to my right and my left. At some distance behind me they followed. The winner of this race would be the man in the best physical condition. I felt confident that I was the man, but I failed to take into account the hand that was bleeding.

I thought as I ran. McKifer does not have his dogs. I've lived in the open for over four years. It will only be a matter of wearing them down. The best plan will be to drop the wire in some hiding place, circle away from our mine and come back later for the wire. This would be simple, but again I had ignored the wounded hand.

All day I traveled, circling at times but moving away from our hideaway and those of other Christians. Repeatedly I heard calls and the firing of a signal gun. I stopped once to drink deeply from the cool water of the creek. By late afternoon fatigue was sitting like a mountain upon my shoulders. With each beat of my heart my hand throbbed. By nightfall I was weak and famished, but all was not lost. Listening, I could no longer hear the enemy. Realizing that I had lost my bearings and could not find my way in the darkness, I crawled into an area of thick undergrowth and slept.

Throughout the night I was awakened by the throbbing of my hand. When morning came, it felt heavy; already there were signs of an angry infection. My face felt hot, my eyes burned, my tongue seemed thick and swollen.

To make matters worse, I knew that I was lost even in the daylight. In the early morning I traveled, slower than yesterday and charting my course by the sun. But this was only guesswork. Constantly I flung a look back along the way that I had come, fearful of seeing or hearing the enemy. My clothes were in tatters, my shoes were cut, and the heat of the sun was oppressive. I was exhausted and sick.

My hand no longer hurt. In fact, there was no feeling at all. It hung swollen and heavy. I found myself extending my tongue, seeking fresh air to cool my hot mouth. I had strayed from the creek and no longer had water to drink. All day I wandered.

In the evening, sick, thirsty, and weak from hunger I sought the shelter of a large rock for the night, hoping it would conceal me from the enemy. I tried to sleep but my body ached, and my groans kept waking me.

Dawn found me faint and dizzy. I struggled to my feet and staggered out of hiding. In an almost stuporous state I was not seeking friends or home; I wanted only water.

By noon if Matt, June, or Cindy had found me, they would have seen a stranger stumbling through the woods, bent, half clothed, supported by a stick in the left hand.

My right hand hung like something dead, but with determination to find water, I moved forward.

The morning dragged on interminably as I staggered aimlessly. Once I drank from a small spring. This was my last water. A dozen times I sank to the ground, too weak to stand, holding my swollen hand that now ached if touched. My body shook with a chill even though the sun was hot. I felt sicker than I knew any man could feel.

By noon hallucinations began to trouble me. I felt confident that I was in a green meadow by a cool stream of water. I fought to clear my mind, but to no avail. I saw Cindy, Matt, and June. I could feel the cool water that bathed my face. I was saved. How wonderful to rest, to be in the hands of friends! My hand no longer aches or feels dead. It has been lanced. I received injections of penicillin. My body has been bathed, and I feel clean. Rich soup is served, and I grow stronger. My friends seem far away, but I can hear them talking. Matt has gone for Uncle Tim. Everything is in hand. I can rest. Blessed rest.

When the moon came up, the dim light found a ragged body lying by a cow trail. By the black, horribly swollen right hand was a pool of dark blood from which a sickening odor arose. The eyes were open but expressionless and dull. The lips moved, but there was no one to hear them. Twice they whispered, "Cindy, Cindy," and then they were still.

Dawn broke with beautiful stillness. Birds fed on the ground. Rabbits hopped unafraid of the ragged body that lay so still.

Uncle Tim had heard the gunshots and the calls of McKifer's men when the pursuit started. He had assumed that McKifer was after me because the sounds of the chase were coming from the direction of my mission. He had gone immediately after Matt.

All day at a safe distance they had stalked McKifer

and his men. In the darkness they, like McKifer, had lost the trail. They knew that I was doomed unless something was done immediately. With morning McKifer would be back with the dogs. The dogs must be killed tonight.

Uncle Tim, Matt, Ben, and Rob met in a council of war. Later Uncle Tim told me how a comment from Ben gave him the answer to the problem. Ben had said, "What we need is the wisdom and courage of a warrior like David."

"David's sling! That's the answer, Ben." Uncle Tim was excited.

"What is?" the rest asked simultaneously.

"Ben, when you were a boy, you were the best sling-shot hunter in town. Can you still shoot?"

"Sure, but what's that got to do with a group of killer dogs?"

Without answering, Uncle Tim turned to Rob. "You, Rob, have the reputation for making the best doughball for fish bait in this area. Right?"

Puzzled but with conviction, Rob defended his reputation. "Yes, sir. My doughballs stay on the line longer and catch more fish, but why this talk of fishing when Steve is on the run?"

"Here's the plan, boys," Uncle Tim answered. Rob was instructed to make heavy doughballs filled with poison. Ben was asked to make the best slingshots that he could construct.

About midnight two men dressed in black, faces and hands blackened with coal dust, left a circle of praying Christians. They made their way down Black Creek to the railroad, turned north, and stayed behind the railroad embankment until they reached the town. There they crossed the railroad and, lying flat on the ground, snaked their way into the shadows of an old store building far enough away from the dog pen to avoid detection. One bark would mean the police and death. Ben felt that he could shoot the poisoned doughballs accurately from that location.

They were near enough to hear the sniffing of inquisitive nostrils as the dogs searched for the strange presence.

Feeling the danger, seeing the black shadows of the store building and hearing nothing in the silent, deserted streets save the restless movement of the dogs, Ben and Rob were stimulated with the courage of fear.

Ben spoke in a whisper, "Rob, hand me a doughball, and keep them coming. I'll keep them going when I start."

They found it easy to shoot every poisoned ball into the dog pen. There were no eyes to see the two shadows as they squirmed along the ground headed for the railroad. Once across the tracks and hidden behind the banks of the railroad bed, they flew over the rough ground. With the relief of those who had teased a lion in his den and escaped, they enjoyed a short burst of hysterical laughter as they ran.

It was 3:00 in the morning when they reached the hiding place of Uncle Tim. All agreed that the dogs would be dead by morning. It was also concluded that I could be hurt and a search should be started now.

As dawn broke with golden rays of light seeking the earth, Uncle Tim, Matt, Ben, and Rob were well into the woods on their search. Having followed the chase at its beginning, it was easy to retrace the route.

The situation had been kept from Cindy and June. Even so, they had suspected danger and had begun preparations for quick medical attention if I were injured. This could have saved my life.

About 9:00 in the morning on the fourth day after I had been shot they found me, more dead than alive. Rob and Ben carried me on a stretcher made out of their coats. By midafternoon we were home, and Cindy was examining me. Blood poisoning had blackened my hand. The arm was hot and swollen to twice its normal size.

Cindy lanced the hand, bathed it with hot water and filled the wound with sulfa powder. The rest of the day and all night she sat by my side.

I defied death and fought for life. At dawn I seemed to overhear a conversation between Uncle Tim and Cindy. Maybe I only remember Uncle Tim telling me about it.

"Uncle Tim," Cindy said, "I've done all that I can do. Steve will be dead by tomorrow unless we get a doctor. Even if he lives, he may lose his arm."

"But Cindy," Uncle Tim replied, "we can't take him to a hospital or doctor. It will be suicide for him and for any of us who take him in. Without the Mark of the Beast no doctor will accept him."

The group sat in silence. Uncle Tim finally spoke:

"Do you remember the men with leprosy who sat at the gate of the city until they were almost starved? One of them said, 'Why sit we here and die?' It's recorded in the Scriptures that they went into the camp of their enemy and found them gone. The camp with all its food belonged to the lepers. I vote to move into the enemy camp.

"I know that going to a doctor or the hospital sounds reckless, but what other option do we have? Only one—stay here and let Steve die. Now hear me out before you say no.

"Although all of the doctors have taken the Mark of the Beast, there is a possibility that the old family physician, Dr. Smithson, will try to save Steve. He attended Steve's mother when Steve was born, and was a close friend of the family. He has his office in his house."

In the early morning they placed me on a stretcher and carried me to the railroad. There they used a hand-car they had "borrowed" to take me to the edge of town. The handcar was hidden and I was carried on the stretcher to Dr. Smithson's house. They placed me on the porch. Then Matt rang the doorbell and slipped away, leaving me in the hands of God and the doctor.

Neither Dr. Smithson nor his nurse, Louise Ray, was too disturbed to hear the doorbell ring at 4:00 in the morning. It took Dr. Smithson, the nurse, and Martha Dodge, the maid, to get me into the house and into Dr. Smithson's examination room.

Nurse Ray discovered my secret as she was preparing me for examination. Sick and only semiconscious, as from a far distance I heard her speak excitedly, "Dr. Smithson,"—the frightened voice seemed to rise above an enormous impediment of speech—"this man is a Christian, an enemy of the state! There's no Economic Mark. If we help him, we're criminals, and we'll all be executed!"

Dr. Smithson turned a little pale around the corners of his mouth. Louise Ray began to tremble, and looked as if she would shriek in sheer terror. Her thin lips formed words that they could not utter. Suddenly the voice began to function.

"That's . . . that's Steve Miles. His whole family were Christians." She drew back as if to touch me meant certain death.

Dr. Smithson, a little shaken but still in command of himself, answered, "Let's forget the man's religion and remember that as a doctor I have taken an oath to minister to the physical needs of men. There are no exceptions."

Neither woman spoke. They knew well that I was a sword suspended over their heads, and that to turn me in was worth $1,000.

After giving me an anesthetic, Dr. Smithson went to work cutting away dead flesh, cleansing the wound, and giving a strong injection of penicillin. The two women worked in silence, but obeyed the doctor's commands.

When the surgery was completed, Dr. Smithson knew

that he had to deal with these ladies. As I was regaining consciousness, I heard him say:

"I have sworn allegiance to the kingdom of the Prince of This World. I'll keep that vow. This man is an enemy. I know Steve and his family. I've been their family doctor all of my professional life. Even so, he has chosen to be an enemy of the government. I'll do what's right tomorrow. Miss Ray, will you keep watch while I get a little more sleep?"

It was gray dawn when Martha Dodge slipped out of the house. Her terror was past, and now malice and greed flickered in her shadowy eyes as she peered back to see if she were being followed. Her direction was toward McKifer's police station. Just for a moment a large black form filled the door of the abandoned post office building that Martha Dodge had to pass. She would have screamed, but a black gloved hand covered her mouth. Her eyes moved wildly and danced in fright, but there was no sound. Ben had done his job well.

Morning found Dr. Smithson attending his patients, but it was also a morning that found his eyes pulled as by a magnet to the back door. Toward noon Nurse Ray came into the room as Dr. Smithson examined me.

"Dr. Smithson." Her eyes were averted. "My brother is sick. I've got to take a few days off." Without waiting for an answer, she was gone.

At dark Dr. Smithson returned to my room to find me some better. Feverish and weak but fully conscious, I remembered much later that I tried to get out of bed but was unable to make it. Dr. Smithson carefully pushed me back down. Shortly after this, his wife came in and gave me some soup. I felt some stronger and very sleepy.

The next thing that I remember was being shaken awake in total darkness. "Steve, Steve," I heard the quiet voice of Dr. Smithson. "Steve, I hate to do this, but I must ask you to leave. I'll give you some medicine to take with you. Before you leave I'll give you a shot to deaden the pain, but you must leave. My housekeeper and nurse are gone. I fear that one of them will report this to the police. Please don't tell me anything. Don't talk. Just leave."

Dr. Smithson helped me out of bed, gave me a pair of old crutches to support me and helped me to the door. His good-bye was short.

"Steve, you were named after me. I've known your family for a long time; but if you're found here, we'll all be killed. Please leave and never return. Take the medicine that I have given you, and you'll be all right."

I was walking weakness as, wincing with pain, I moved slowly across the porch. I slipped on a smooth step, and nearly fell, but recovered myself.

Weak and unused to crutches, I moved grotesquely down the sidewalk toward the railroad. Too sick to be watchful and careful, I stubbed my foot on a loose rock and fell. Although I instinctively tried to protect my right side, the jar started pains in the wounded hand. They moved remorselessly up my arm to burst into a tidal wave of agony and nausea over the whole body. I lay panting on my side. The nausea caused me to shake as with a chill. Although they were only a few feet away, I could not reach the crutches. I struggled for them as well as a dying man is supposed to struggle.

For the second time since I had been shot, hallucinations began to trouble me. The sidewalk was only a few feet away. I had walked it hundreds of times as a child. Tonight I could hear the laughter of children. I saw them and tried to join them. But each time I reached out to grasp their hands, the pain brought me back to consciousness.

Then I heard voices. Two dark figures moved through

the night. It was Ben and Rob. I think that I wept with joy. I fought the delusion, trying to bring myself back to reality. But how easy to yield to the pleasure of being lifted onto the stretcher. Very quickly they carried me through the night. "Oh, yes! we're the people of the night." I laughed at the thought. A hand closed over my mouth and a voice whispered, "Steve, be quiet."

Oh, lovely delusion. We are on the handcar, sailing smoothly toward the cave of the Christians. People of the night. Men of the underground.

Tangled thoughts tumbled through my sick mind. I'll tell Uncle Tim about Dr. Smithson. Here they come. There's Cindy floating through the air in long bounds that defy gravity. How concerned her look. How fresh her hair. How do Cindy and June manage to appear so clean and fresh all of the time when they live in a coal mine?

How my hand hurts. It's getting dark. Cindy, Cindy, I can't see you. Where did you go? I'm so thirsty. McKifer will find me in the morning. We are people of the night. Death is my appointment. The grave is my refuge. I am so sick.

My body twitched in pain, and I groaned in agony. The suffering seemed unbearable. The total sickness settled in my throbbing head.

The first thing I remember clearly was lying on a cot in the sun. Cindy was sitting by me. Summer was gone because the trees were turning. Within a few minutes Cindy had recounted the details of my illness. For the next weeks I received the constant care of Cindy, Matt, and June. At the end of a month I was walking.

# 6

# Death Watch

*There was given unto him a great sword* (Rev. 6:4).

During the days of my recovery, I watched the development of world events almost incessantly. The news was filled with reports and scenes of the killing of Christians. Some were reported to the police by members of their own family. Others were taken in police raids.

One horrible scene was of a group of Christians found in the basement of an old farm house. The house was simply burned on top of them. When some tried to climb out through windows, soldiers threw them back. The news reporters had recorded their dying screams and they had moved the cameras in close for a full and complete report on the burning Christians.

It was the kind of coverage that was once given to sporting events. The raid had taken place at night. In the broken darkness of firelight I could see the dazed horror on the faces of men and women as they crowded around windows. I saw them pleading with fluttering hands. I heard them—some whimpering, some with savage cries and others prayed. The camera moved from window to window. Newsmen seemed to take excessive care to be sure that no scene was missed. The camera stopped on an elderly couple who clutching each other, stood at a window, framed by fire and smoke. They gave a long, frightened gaze at the crowd of spectators and then fell back into the burning building.

With a tone of victory, the announcer told of thousands of Christians being imprisoned and executed. The World Peace Bureau reported that it was their goal to exterminate all signs of Christianity from the earth within six months.

The news was followed by a report from the world ruler himself, Prince Goldbar. It was obvious that he no longer pretended to be kind or fatherly. He was the stern, unemotional ruler of the world. He spoke forceably and with malice. His eyes burned with hate, but not blindly. The set of his face bespoke a silent doom to all Christians. His face was the incarnation of menace, and behind all the malice there was an expression of something satanic.

Goldbar's message was specific. Orders had previously been given to exterminate all Christians. But tonight he announced,

"Each government and each officer will be held personally responsible for the presence of any Christians found in his area. Any family protecting a Christian will be put to death along with the Christians. Any neighbor who does not report suspicious conduct in his community will be held accountable for any Christian that may be found there. In the future few, if any, Christians will die alone. Those who do not report known Christians will die with the traitors whom they protect."

This was a declaration of worldwide killing and the fulfillment of the Scripture, "They shall kill one another with a great sword" (Rev. 6:4). Tribulation Christians had been killed by the thousands; now they would be killed by the millions.

Day after day the news was filled more and more with pictures and reports of the killing of Christians. The more gruesome the killing, the greater the glee the news media seemed to find in showing all of the details.

"Matt, Steve! Come quickly! Hurry!" June and Cindy called in chorus.

Matt and I rushed into the mine to find them staring in horror at the television set. The scene was from a sports stadium in Italy. As I arrived at the set, a young couple was being led into the arena. The announcer reported:

"Ladies and gentlemen, the young couple now entering will be escorted to the center of the arena. At that point they will turn and face Prince Goldbar. They will be given the opportunity to pledge allegiance to the Alliance of the World and to the Prince of This World."

When the couple turned to face Goldbar the camera brought the faces in clearly. They were pale with fear and the microphone picked up the voices. An officer standing by them spoke.

"Do you, Anthony Marcus, and you, Elvinia Antonio, renounce the deceitfulness of the Christian faith and the Leader, Jesus Christ? Do you repent of your error in the name of the savior of this world, Prince Goldbar? If so, say, 'I do.'"

The answer came clearly from both of them; "I do."

The officer continued, "You will repeat the pledge of allegiance after me, and then you will be given the world Economic Mark. First, the pledge."

"I pledge allegiance to the Alliance of the World and to the Prince of This World, who is the one and only true ruler and savior. This is a government indivisible, with blessings and pleasures for all men now and forever. In the Prince I trust."

Following the pledge a number was stamped upon the backs of their hands. My attention was immediately called to Prince Goldbar. Trumpets sounded, and flags were raised. There was the white flag and the beast with ten horns. But it was not the flag that caught my attention; it was the banner across the front of the box where Prince Goldbar stood. On the banner were the huge numbers 666.

When Prince Goldbar spoke it was his usual political emphasis on how much he cared for the people, and how much he wanted all the needs of men everywhere to be met. But the last part of his speech was different. It was the fulfillment of a prophecy that had perplexed men for ages. He spoke slowly and distinctly.

"And now, my fellow citizens, it is my pleasure to announce that the symbol of my government is being changed from the white horse with a rider holding the bow but with no arrows. This is no longer meaningful. We are at war with a radical, deceitful enemy called Christians. They are now claiming that the so-called 'resurrected and raptured saints' will return with angels and that the crucified Man called Jesus will take over my kingdom. If they seek war, then I say, Away with peace. We will have war!

"The Christians who see the error of their way, accept the Economic Mark, and pledge allegiance to my government will live. But those who continue to oppose me will die. We have hunted the traitors by police, but now all the power of the Alliance of the World is dedicated to the extermination of every sign of Christianity.

"From this day on, the symbol of my government will be the symbol of man. The number 6 has stood for man through the ages. This is a government of the people and not of the gods. It is a threefold government: for the people, by the people, and of the people. Therefore, the number 6, the symbol for man, shall be the symbol of this government threefold—666.

"The people called Christians are not citizens. They are inhuman, creatures of the night, animals of the dark and underground. They will be treated as animals. Tonight you will be entertained by these rebellious, degraded creatures. Their own Book teaches that they will die 'with the beasts of the earth.'[1] I would not want them to lose faith in their own Book.

"Ladies and gentlemen, tonight I give the world the opportunity to see Christians fight the wild beasts as their fathers did in the earliest days of this revolutionary band."

The cameras turned again to the arena. The young couple who had recanted were gone. In their place stood 12 men and women. From the opposite side of the arena a dozen cages were being pulled toward the Christians. How lonely they looked, how helpless, and how doomed! Now I could clearly hear the snarls of angry dogs. The trucks stopped. The cage doors opened. Two dozen or more ferocious dogs bounded straight toward the Christians and began to circle them.

The men quickly surrounded the women, as the cameras focused on one large dog. The muscles of the huge body contracted spasmodically. There was a savage violence that made the animal horrible to see. He crouched low, his eyes blazing with menace.

Then it happened. Growling with rage and savage violence, the big dog sprang. This was some kind of signal to the entire band. All the stored up savage nature in them drove them as they attacked. We all heard the loud, savage snarls. We saw the wild, fiery eyes of the beasts. We saw clearly the white fangs, cutting and slashing at the Christians.

Wild cries of horror came from June and Cindy.

---

1. Rev. 6:8.

107

Matt's lips were a thin, straight line, his eyes cold and emotionless. I felt hot and angry. I hated our feeling of helplessness.

But we saw something else: the Christians fought. Previously, I had viewed them as lonely, weak, and doomed. They did not seem to see themselves that way. These people without earthly friends to encourage them, without one face in the arena to show pity, stood taller than Prince Goldbar and all of his kingdom. Death may well have placed his hand upon them, but death would not take them easily.

There was the cushioned sounds of fists as men struck the flesh of dogs. There was a struggle of deadly intensity. Men were bleeding, but I saw dogs flung through the air as if propelled from a cannon.

Suddenly, I realized that we were all on our feet. June's voice sounded thin in my ears, but she was crying, "Come on! Come on! Come on!" Cindy was looking incredulously at the screen and in a voice neither high nor low was saying, "How brave! How strong! What people!" Matt's lips were saying nothing, but in his eyes there was a triumphant gleam. Where did those men get such courage and strength? The women fought too.

Not one person in the Christian band was seen to cower or heard to whimper. The moment of death for the Christians would come, because though the dogs were hurled back, they attacked again. The arms of all the men bled, and the faces of some were gashed. The fighting was no mere flare of gallantry; it was a battle against the evils of hell itself.

Just as I saw the first man about to go down, the camera focused on him. His fingers were locked on the throat of a huge dog, and the teeth of the dog were sunk in the man's shoulder. How silent the struggle. I felt my body shiver. Still the camera was locked on the man's face.

I saw the veins stand out in his neck. I saw the individual drops of perspiration. I saw the muscles of the face strain as he fought. The camera switched. Then I knew why. The man was falling. A second beast was biting, jerking, and tearing at his left leg.

As he fell, a third dog leaped at his throat. I saw the legs of the fallen man kick spasmodically, and then there was only the movement of the body being jerked by the dogs.

The crowd had gone wild with joy at the fall of the first Christian. Now that the circle of fighting men was broken, others fell rapidly.

One of the women turned and gave the camera a long steady look. There were no tears in her eyes. No words were formed on her lips. She only gazed. She was torn and bloody, but the eyes were strong and undefeated. A sad smile swept across the face, and she was gone.

The broken bodies of the 12 Christians were strewn about the arena by the dogs. They had died bravely. Not one of the 12 had tried to save himself by denying his Christ.

The reporters advised all viewers to stay tuned for the review of specials from around the world. These would be presented by the News Bureau of the Alliance as a warning to any traitor, and for the pleasure of all who loved the Prince and his government.

The first scenes that we watched forced us to ask, "How could this happen? What has gone wrong with the civilized world?" I knew the truth, but the truth was hard to accept.

The pictures came from all over the world. Ordinary citizens were forcing neighbors to write "Christian" on the doors of their houses; then the Christians were dragged away. Churches were either set on fire, or new names were written on them. One had a new name in bright red letters,

"Christian Brothel." Frightened girls standing in front were held captive by soldiers. Their blouses were pulled back so that the numbers 666 could be seen. These Christian girls were forced into government brothels for a time and then killed.

The second picture came from the Ruhr Corporation that had built the cremation ovens for Hitler. They presented their latest models. These were not powered by gas, but by laser beams. A thousand bodies could be turned into ashes in minutes.

The world was given a demonstration. A large group of men and women were stripped naked before the world. This was followed by the sound of a trumpet and the roll of drums. A grinning soldier handed one Christian a flag with a cross on it. The boy took the flag and and began to sing "Onward Christian Soldiers." The Christians did march. Some hand in hand, but no fainting. There was no crying. They marched into the crematorium oven. The doors were closed. Within five minutes it was over. When the doors were opened the ovens looked clean. The bodies of the Christians had simply been turned into nothing by the laser beams.

The third group of pictures showed torture by more old-fashioned methods. In one picture 20 young women had their shoes removed, and blowtorches applied to their feet. They were told to curse Jesus Christ and live. No one cursed. In the next picture men and women were seen hanging from light posts and trees along the street. Signs attached to their bodies read, "Death to the Christians."

In our mine home we could talk only in whispers. Then we became quiet. Long we gazed in stupified silence. Not a sound.

Uncle Tim's arrival brought us back to activity. He knew of the worldwide killings, but he also knew of a renewed danger for us. His bottle contact from Ray's

Bridge reported that a search sweep of our area by the police would take place within a week. We had to move.

Ben and Rob rounded up four horses and would be ready to move us the following night. We had one night and a day in which to pack.

"Uncle Tim," I asked, "what about the other Christians?"

"They all know," he answered. "Some are moving tonight. In this emergency some will move in daylight through heavy woods tomorrow. It's best that we move in small groups."

Ben and Rob knew the county well. It was decided that our group would travel by night and hide by day. Ben and Rob would act as guides. We were to travel north where our new hiding place would be a rugged area in a large government forest. It would take five nights of hard marching to cover the 100 miles.

After a day of packing, we were ready. With some emotion we left our home of almost two years. The four horses were heavily loaded, but, even so, much of our food was left behind. This troubled us, because we estimated that at least two years of the Tribulation were left. However, our priorities called for medicine, tools, clothing, and food in that order. Television sets were left, but radios were taken.

We settled down for a hot dinner because we knew that our strength would be taxed by the next five days. Uncle Tim had gone ahead to pick out a homesite. Only Rob and Ben knew exactly where he had gone.

As darkness came, Ben was the first to detect trouble. The north wind was icy and rising, but it was the rain that spelled trouble.

"Steve, Matt," Ben's voice sounded calm but factual. "We may be in for trouble. Heavy clouds are moving in fast. We've given ourselves five nights to make the trip but

111

if the rain continues, we can't stop as often as we'd planned. For one thing, there won't be a dry place to rest. And secondly we'll be crossing Black Creek in several places and will have to ford the stream. It's too dangerous to cross on the bridges. If the creek rises, we'll have to make all the crossings before it floods."

We left in the dark and in a pouring rain. Soon our clothing was soaked in spite of our rainwear. The north wind became a personal enemy as it stung our faces. Then the wind began psychological warfare. Back in the night-blackened hills it began in a low distant moan and rushed at us, growing louder until the unearthly sounds were enough to test the nerves of the strongest. At the same time the rain whipped at our eyes, hit at our faces, and seeped down our collars.

Rob walked by the lead horse, June and Matt by the second, Cindy and I by the third, and Ben by the fourth. We traveled single file.

I became concerned about Cindy falling as we walked in the wet, black night—so dark that Rob had to lead by instinct and not by sight.

"Cindy," I said softly.

"Yes, Steve," her answer was just as soft.

"Hold to the horse's bridle. This will keep you from falling if you should stumble."

"You're late with that advice," she replied. Her voice sounded cheerful in spite of the darkness, cold, and rain. "I've been leaning on this horse almost from the start."

Stumbling through the darkness, I too walked with one hand on the horse's harness. Often my eyes closed against the cold. My thoughts ran deep.

How I wished that I had taken time to know Cindy in normal days. Why had I spent my life in selfish ambition? It was pride, not hunger for truth, that had robbed me of my faith, my family, and the Rapture.

The wind rushing through trees and around rocks made a variety of sounds. There were long wailings like the cry of a lost child. Others were deep and rumbling like the echoes from some unearthly pit. I felt that I could stand the rain and cold well enough if the wild wailing of the wind would cease. The shrieks were torture.

It must have been near midnight when Cindy called: "Steve how is your hand? How is your strength holding up?"

"I'm doing just great, Cindy. How are you doing on this horse express?"

Even here, her humor held up. "Not too well, Steve. The travel is just too fast. The bright lights hurt my eyes, and the seats are so soft that I get sleepy."

I laughed in spite of the rain and cold. In the blackness I found Cindy's hand and gripped it.

"Hold on little girl. We'll make it to the Millennium yet!"

What had I said? "We'll make it into the Millennium!" A strong surge of confidence swept through me that it could be done and, with God's help, I intended to do it. Not only that, but I intended to take Cindy with me.

From that moment I had a new purpose in survival. What a thought! One thousand years with Cindy in the Millennium! For the first time in my life I had the feeling that I was in love, but it was a love that could not be told or shared. Not in the Tribulation.

Sometime before dawn, fatigue began to set in, and my mind jumped from one thing to another. Most of my thoughts were about the night—black enough to make Cindy almost invisible within arm's length! A night of cold rain and wind. Still we walked.

Dawn came, pale and ominous. With daylight came new causes for fear. Where were we? Only Ben and Rob knew. Would the lack of sleep make them careless? Would McKifer and his men be on the prowl?

There was no sun. The gray sky and earth were touched by prowling snowflakes. This would be a day of cold and dampness.

Then I saw an old farmhouse. It was evident that it had been abandoned for a long time. The roof was half caved in, trees and grass were tall around it. But with the straightforwardness of a man who knew his directions, Rob guided us through a door into the roofed side.

"Say, Rob, it's lucky that we found this. We can rest here until night." Matt was expressing more of a wish than making a statement of fact.

"Well, Matt, your observation is good, but there are two errors. Coming here is not luck. Uncle Tim has had us working for months to mark out routes for retreat. We're here by planning and not by luck. But we can't stay more than an hour. It's too dangerous. When McKifer comes this way, he searches every shelter. We had intended to rest in a thick undergrowth of bushes, but it is too wet and cold. We'll eat here, rest for an hour and move on."

Again I was thankful for Uncle Tim. It seemed that he always had an answer before the crisis. What a leader! Then too, Ben and Rob were prizes. They never seemed to be excited. Whatever the subject, they talked in the same calm, relaxed voice.

Evidently I dozed. The next thing I heard was Rob calling, "All aboard for the horse express." I may have been only half awake, but I knew that something was different. However, there was no time to think or ask questions. We were moving out.

Then I knew. The wind was not blowing, and we stepped out into a day of fog. We had exchanged the blanket of blackness for a sheet of whiteness. During the night Ben and Rob had tied the horses together so that there was no chance for one to stray in the darkness. We still needed that protection.

Late in the morning the sun broke through for a moment. But it was no more than a pale light casting feeble rays upon the earth which lay enveloped in a wet whiteness.

Rocks and trees held the coldness they had gathered from the night, and offered only chilliness for the day. I did not feel rested. The hour we had stopped could not renew the strength drained from a night's forced march. I knew from my war experience that the day would bring more fatigue, and tired people are tempted to be careless people. We must be careful.

All morning we traveled. In the army, regulations called for two and a half miles per hour with a 10-minute break each hour. We had hoped to do better than this with the horses carrying our load. However, we had not expected the rain.

Later the rain began again. This did away with our protective fog, and I requested a halt in the cover of dwarf pines.

"We're in trouble." I tried to make my voice sound factual but not fearful. "Rob, it's dangerous to travel so exposed. Don't McKifer and his men hunt this area?"

"They sure do, Steve. They have maps that mark every trail and hiding place in this part of the state."

"That's what I feared. Why don't we hide in the bushes even if we are forced to sit in the rain?"

"Steve,"—here was the unemotional Rob talking as calmly as if he were discussing a fishing trip—"if this rain continues, we must ford Black Creek before dark. It's dangerous to travel in daylight because of the police, but the flood waters may be a greater danger than McKifer."

I agreed with Rob but offered another suggestion.

"I understand the danger of the flood, but McKifer

115

is also a real danger. Since we must travel by day, tired and in the rain, we may be careless. Someone should precede the main party by at least a half mile. We still have one shotgun. The leader should take the gun, and if there is an ambush, try to get off one shot as a signal to the others."

"Good idea, Steve. At this point Ben and I are the only ones who know the route. Give me a 15-minute start, and Ben can lead this group. The fact is, no one will have any problem following a trail in this mud."

We had all missed a night's sleep. It was a weary party that moved out. We traveled without speech, saving our breath for walking. What the others thought, I don't know. For me, it was a temptation to believe that all of this was a nightmare.

We traveled all day, eating cold food as we walked or during 10-minute rest stops. Ben laid our course by the muddy tracks left by Rob's horse. The forest seemed interminable. The icy, freezing rain continued.

By nightfall we were fatigued, footsore, and famishing. The thought of crossing the creek and then finding shelter, food, and rest urged us on. But thoughts of food and rest did not relieve me of fear. If we could follow Rob's trail so easily, McKifer and his men could follow ours. I found myself looking back in constant dread of being discovered. This thought must have been in the minds of the others also. I observed Cindy as she flung a look over the road that we had traveled and often glanced to the right or left.

Now we were working our way down toward the creek which had become a river. Ben went in first, leading his horse. As Cindy and I started into the water, I reminded her to keep a firm hold on the horse. The horses were surefooted but a little nervous. Waist deep, we waded into the frigid water. Teeth chattering and shoulders shaking with cold, we made a headlong rush to free ourselves of the icy stream. Slipping on smooth rocks, we hurried up the muddy banks to the pine trees where Ben was waiting.

As we approached Ben, I noticed Cindy limping. "Cindy, what happened?"

"I turned my ankle . . ." She never finished.

The roar of a shotgun in the distance flooded us with terror. Immediately a chain of shots followed.

Ben went into action with rapid-fire commands. "Head north! Keep on all night! Don't stop again until it is day! Don't stop to eat although you're hungry! I'm sure that the first shot was from Rob. Cross back over the creek, and keep on north. This will take longer to get to our destination, but it will be safer. I'll find you on the trail. Here, Steve, take my horse." With that Ben was gone. I did not know it then, but I was to see Ben and Rob only one more time.

"Matt, the faster we move, the safer. Hold onto the horse, Cindy, and we'll go first."

We were soon across the creek without difficulty. When we came out on the other side, I noticed that Cindy was limping badly.

"Here, let me look at that ankle."

"Oh, Steve, there's nothing wrong. I turned it a little when I slipped on a rock. There's no real problem."

When she tried to demonstrate how well she could walk, she winced with pain. We had to act. There was no time to discuss options.

"Matt, you and June move out. We'll follow in a few minutes." It was almost as if out of the darkness we all heard the sound of alarm.

"Steve, take care." Matt gripped my hand. June kissed my cheek, gave Cindy a quick hug and they were lost in the darkness of the forest.

Quickly I untied and lifted two large bundles off the

largest horse. I pulled a dry blanket from under the plastic, lifted a protesting Cindy on the horse, and we were on our way. Shivering in the cold night wind, worried and wondering what had happened to Rob and, by now, to Ben, we moved into the night.

Dimly we could see that we were following an old cow trail now under an inch or two of water. How long we traveled in this silence I don't know. Fatigue was drugging my body. The cold was numbing, getting into my lungs, deadening my face, hands, and wet feet. The water on the ground was freezing. The crunch of ice came up clearly.

The blanket protected Cindy, and walking kept me from freezing. If the horse jerked the rope in my hand, sharp pains shot through my arm, and my fingertips tingled with pin-piercing pain. The world about us was hostile. We were strangers in an alien land. There was only black, wet desolation and cold loneliness.

There was no haughty spirit left in Steve Miles tonight. No mockery of God's Word. No show-off spirit of pseudo-intellectualism. There was only a cold, wet, hungry man moving with a weary gait up the slope toward the black sky.

Nothing to say. Nothing to see. Just rain and a cold north wind blowing in my face. I found some refuge in the memories of my youth. I saw the color of the grapes that grew on the fence by the house. I could smell the odor of the apples that filled the cellar. I found myself wishing Cindy could have shared all those childhood experiences with me.

My dreaming was brought to a sudden halt by a hushed but urgent call from Cindy, "Steve, look!"

After one day and two nights without sleep, I thought I was suffering from hallucinations. Directly in front of us was a fire. It may have been a quarter of a mile ahead, but it was a fire.

Then began as serious a drama as was ever played. If this were McKifer and his men, they were watching for a southern approach. But if Matt and June, Rob or Ben had been taken, I could not just move off and leave them. I began to circle north. When well north of the fire, Cindy and I held a quick council of war. She would stay with the horses and be ready for a quick getaway.

Carefully I moved through the wet grass toward the fire. Remembering my military training, I scooped up mud to camouflage my face. As I came closer, I crawled through water toward some large rocks in a grove of pine trees. There I would be able to see without being seen. I tried to be no more than a shadow. On hands and knees, every sense alert, I moved noiselessly toward the rocks and trees.

From my hiding place I began to explore the campsite. What I saw filled me with horror and left me feeling helpless. There were June, Matt, and Rob by the fire. Their arms were tied behind them. They appeared unhurt. Where was Ben? Had he been killed?

Four of McKifer's men were in view. They were drinking and talking loudly. I crawled nearer to the shelter of a tree and rock. The three captives stood side by side. To their right were the four policemen. McKifer was not one of them.

The situation was getting more serious by the minute as the policemen became more intoxicated. They were grinning and eyeing June with sensual greed. Matt and Rob said nothing, but a fierce defiance could be seen in the flash of their eyes. In their faces was the righteous violence of those who protect what they love.

One of the men called smirkingly, "Say, Christian, let's have a nice little party, private like." He put his gun down and moved toward June. There was a wolfish gleam on his face. The other three policemen were still busy with the bottles.

It was only then I realized that something else was taking place. Rob had slowly moved farther to the left away from the police. Also something was squirming along the ground toward the fire, carefully keeping the bodies of the captives between him and the police. It was Ben. He reached Rob. In one movement he cut Rob's ropes and grabbed the man moving toward June. Rob quickly freed Matt and June.

From that point it would be impossible for me to describe what happened event by event. Ben lifted the policeman into the air and flung him against a pine tree. His scream was horrible. The remaining three policemen threw down their bottles; one reached for his gun. He never made it. I hurled a boulder that weighed at least five pounds at him. I heard a scream, and someone was rolling on the ground. I saw Ben, Rob, and Matt leap at the remaining policemen, but I also saw someone emerging from the dark. Then clearly I saw the face of McKifer. It was in a scowl—his eyes pitiless, the set of his jaws hard. His whole face was malignant with hate. Here was one who killed with joy.

Even as his gun began to blaze, I was running toward June. Where it came from I can't be sure, but I heard a savage cry of anger followed by the sound of a struggle of deadly intensity. It was impossible to know what was going on in the mass confusion and desperation.

Pulling June as I ran, I vaguely saw men lying on the ground, men fighting. I heard groans and the continued sound of a gun that meant men were dying.

Still pulling June, I ran, knowing that above all things I had to get her away. More important than being careful was getting far from here as quickly as possible. Stumbling over rocks, limbs and bushes tearing at me, I held onto June and ran frantically toward the area where Cindy waited. I shuddered at the thought of those beast-like men

120

getting their hands on Cindy or June. There was no time for explanation. Quickly I lifted a protesting June on the horse with Cindy.

"Girls, hold on. We must make all the time we can while it is still dark. Remember, dead or alive, you're worth $1,000 each to anyone who wishes to turn you over to the government."

With this, I leaped on the second horse, and we were off at a fast walk headed north. We could not run the horses in the thick trees.

The remainder of the night we traveled, laying our course north by intuition. Unaccustomed to riding, my thighs were soon stiff and aching. After a few hours in the cold, the pain was replaced by numbness. I had to reach down and touch my legs in order to locate them. I knew that I had to find shelter. Neither the girls, nor I, nor the animals could keep this up. We had been on the move almost without a break for two nights and a day.

Dawn came with a ghostly, gray mist. Trees and rocks seemed reluctant to assume their shapes, remaining diffused and concealed. The dampness and the cold conspired to clutch at our bodies, penetrate our bones, and leave us shivering and lost.

Suddenly the horses stopped and brought me back to full alertness. We were on the steep banks of a stream. I assumed it was Black Creek. The girls sat on the horses like statues, unmoving, with heads bowed. Silently but earnestly I prayed,

"O God what can I do? Where can we go?"

Surely God stimulated my mind. It was almost as if a voice spoke, "Remember your military training. Blend in with the environment. Become a part of nature. Make the earth your ally."

Then I saw a leaf-covered path leading down toward the creek. I left the horses to follow the trail. Soon I was picking my way through heavy underbrush along a narrow path that descended sharply to the creek banks. This was not a man-made trail but a path used by wild animals. The horses could be coaxed down here. About 100 yards up the creek was an overhanging rock that would give us shelter. This would be as good a place as any to make our stop for the day. The path leading down to the creek was well hidden, and, once under the rock, we could not be seen from above or from the opposite side of the creek. Here we would be concealed from any prying eyes by thick undergrowth and rocks.

Returning to the girls I found them unmoved. I called softly, "Cindy, June."

They responded immediately, but both appeared unutterably weary. "Yes, Steve," they answered in voices reflecting the last stages of exhaustion.

"I've found a refuge for the day. I don't believe McKifer and his men are following us; but if they are, we'll be safe here."

Remembering her sprained ankle, I said, "Cindy, I'll get a crutch to help you walk." This was easy in the heavily wooded area. I was careful, however, not to cut or break limbs. We must leave no signs for anyone to follow. I led the lead horse, Cindy came hobbling after me, and June led the second horse. The wet leaves made our journey a silent one.

Within minutes we were under our shelter. Wind-blown leaves, blessed dry leaves, gave us a carpet. The bank and rocks protected us from the wind and rain. I was extremely weary and wished to lie down to sleep, but necessity demanded action.

I retraced the trail to wipe out signs of our descent. The wet leaves covered our tracks well. I picked up broken limbs and dropped them in the path. It would have taken an expert tracker to find us.

When I returned to the hiding place, I made a small fire of dry twigs. There was no smoke. From the horses' packs we got cans of meat and beans. The hot food and warm fire induced fatigue and demanded sleep. We unfolded blankets and slept the sleep of the exhausted.

When I awoke, rain was falling. The brief day had come and gone. Evening was upon us.

My first duty was to get the fire started. The second obligation was more complex. How could I tell the girls that we were lost? Matt, Ben, and Rob were probably dead. I had no idea where we could find Uncle Tim and the other Christians even if they were still alive.

The fire was kept small; only a few twigs at a time. It was June who spoke first as we gathered around the tiny blaze.

"Steve, are we going back to look for the others?"

This was a question that had haunted me. My emotions said, "Go back and look." My intelligence dictated, "Run."

"June," I said, "if they escaped, they are all able to take care of themselves. The most pressing obligation I have now is to get you two as far away from here as possible."

For the second time we heated cans of food. After eating, we all prayed for our friends, asking God for their deliverance. I dared not mention it to the girls, but time after time the scripture came to me, "I saw the souls of them that were beheaded for the witness of Jesus, and for the Word of God, and which had not worshipped the beast" (Rev. 20:4).

No other words were spoken. We sat by the fire awaiting the night.

# 7

## Lost

*When he had opened the third seal, I heard the
third beast say, Come and see. And I beheld, and
lo a black horse; and he that sat on him had a pair of
balances in his hand* (Rev. 6:5).

We all wore dark clothing. I took charcoal from the fire
and blackened our faces. We were each mindful of the
danger, the darkness, and our lostness as we slowly moved
out of our camp.

All night we traveled north. There was no moon. Just
darkness. Nowhere did I discover a break in the heavens,
not even one star. I was terrified. What if we met the
police? What would happen to June and Cindy? I recalled
with horror the lustful expression of the policeman as he
had stalked toward June. I prayed as I had never prayed in
all my life for divine guidance and for strength to save
these girls.

In the darkness of the night, time gets lost. Hours drag
on eternally. Hope evades one's grasp. In this depressed
mood I suddenly realized that I could see in the dark. For
five years I had been in hiding, and the major part of my
active time had been at night. It was surprising how well I

could see even when I complained about the darkness. Even so, I walked by the head of the lead horse and let him choose the path. I chose only the direction, north.

At first, every 30 minutes I stopped to listen. But there was only the silence of the woods broken by the dripping rain from the trees. Wet and tired, I stared into the night, and moved toward its unknown embrace cautiously. We traveled, but where were we going? There was a rendez-vous, but where?

We needed a place to hide. In daylight an unseen pair of binoculars might be trained upon us. The risk of a chance meeting with a traveler or of approaching a road before we detected it was too great. I estimated that it was an hour or more before day when I began to pray earnestly and to look for a place of concealment.

We were deep in the national forest, and we needed not only a place to hide for this day, we needed a home. It was time to stop running. We needed to dig in for the remaining years of the Tribulation.

Day was breaking, wet and uninviting, when I noticed a change. We had emerged from the pine trees into an apple orchard; not a cultivated orchard but old, gnarled, half-dead trees. The long night's walk had left me dazed and groggy, but the realization of being in an orchard made me cautious. Some place out there in the semi-darkness there must be a house. I felt a prickling fear at the back of my neck and in the tightness of my shoulders. My first impulse was to retreat into the woods. But then, maybe this was an abandoned house. It could be what we were looking and praying for.

I led the horses into a thick hedge growth. "Girls," I called softly.

"Yes, Steve," they answered together.

"You two stay here with the horses. I'm going to scout the area for a place to stay for the day."

"Be careful, Steve. For your sake and for ours," Cindy whispered.

"Don't worry. I will be."

I had walked less than 200 yards when I saw an old house, lonely like some broken and abandoned toy. It was falling into decay, and the sun bleached walls looked damp and cold in the thin morning light.

For a full 30 minutes I watched from my hiding place. Moving with caution, I almost glided from the brush concealment. Crouching as close to the ground as possible, I was nearly invisible as I approached the house. Not until I stood by the walls did I take a deep breath. Step by cautious step, I approached the window, stopping to look and listen. Like some animal of the forest, I tried to detect an enemy by sensing the wind. Nothing moved. No sound came.

Gliding along the wall, I came to a window. Neither shades nor curtains covered it. Looking in, I saw a dusty, abandoned house. Remaining alert for any suspicious sound or movement, I went to the door that stood open and walked through the house. It had evidently been unoccupied for a long time.

I returned for the girls, leaving the horses tied in the heavy growth. Again we stopped some distance from the house. Here in the heavy growth we commanded a full view of the area. We stood quietly, watching and knowing well that to make a mistake might be to die. Now we moved into the yard, alert, and cautious, but the silence in the cold world around us was complete.

The house had been unused for years and there were no signs of anyone coming for even an occasional visit. It had the appearance of having been occupied and then suddenly deserted.

"Look, Steve," June called softly, "over here." By the old stone fireplace was a rocker and a table. On the table were a faded Bible and a pair of glasses. The Bible was opened to the Christmas story.

"You know what I think?"

"I can guess, Steve," Cindy answered. "Someone who lived here read the Christmas story, and retired for the night to be raptured away before day."

Even though the house was empty and had been for years, we concluded it would be too dangerous to stay here through the day. Back with the horses and our provisions, cans of food were opened and eaten cold. We lay down on plastic, covered ourselves and tried to sleep through the day.

In the early evening, June and Cindy stayed with the horses while I went out before total darkness to explore our new area carefully. I circled the buildings watching for anything that would tell me about the place. As I stood deep in the shadows, I saw signs that meant there was no immediate danger. A squirrel was eating nuts on the front porch, and a deer was grazing in the yard. This gave me courage to step boldly into the clearing.

I found one thing of special interest, something that I would never have observed before the Tribulation days and my living with nature. There was a faint' path leading from the house to the barn. That was not unusual, but the path continued from the barn toward the woods and a hill that I saw in the distance. I made up my mind to follow this path later.

I joined Cindy and June at the camp for an unappetizing meal of cold beans. Reporting my finding of the path, I declared my determination to be up at first dawn to explore the area in detail. The farm seemed as safe as any place we could find. The only road was an old logging trail. There were no power lines. This had indeed been an isolated farm.

Sitting on plastic sheets, and wrapped in blankets, we

sat in the dark talking. For the second time June spoke of Matt.

"Steve, what do you think happened to Matt and the others? If Matt is dead, I hope that God permitted him to die quickly."

"June," I answered honestly, "I don't know. From the sound of the guns I would have to assume that Matt, Ben, and Rob are in heaven."

"You know," June continued, "it is strange how human nature makes us assume that these things can't happen to us. When I read in the Bible of the killings in the time of the Tribulation, it was always someone else. Not me; not my family."

Our conversation was silenced by the hooting of an owl. That was music to us. If McKifer or others were on our trail, the world of the wild would be silent.

We all prayed and settled down for the night. As bad as our condition was, we had much to be thankful for. We were dry and warm, and we had food. Cindy's ankle was better.

At daylight, I was on the trail from the barn toward the hill. The beauty of the winter morning, the brisk air, and the songs of the birds challenged the truth that the earth was bleeding and dying.

I had not followed the trail far before I knew that someone had made an effort to hide it. The path twisted, crossed a small stream of water and crossed back again. Most of the twisting trail had disappeared years ago under a layer of pine needles. Even so, because of heavy use in the past it had worn into the ground and I was able to follow it.

Now the path turned sharply upward toward the hill and thick pine trees. I picked my way through heavy undergrowth and climbed the steep hill. The path left the heavy, bushy area and the trees became thicker.

For years now I had lived close to nature, and I could not help but laugh aloud as I thought of the change that had taken place in me. Here was the proud Dr. Stephen Miles, professor of New Testament literature, following an old trail through the woods as if his life depended on it. And very well three lives may have depended on it. In these five years since the Rapture I had changed considerably. I understood nature better. I was competent as a man of the night. I could follow a trail that five years before I would have crossed without even seeing it.

Dwarf pines were thick on the hillside. The path led me deeper into this enclosing shelter. The trail came to a sudden end against a gray boulder as large as a house. Pine trees and vines were thick around the rock. Why would a path lead here? Working my way through the trees and the vines, I circled the boulder.

There was my answer. Behind the rock was a cave. Just a little exploring revealed the cave to be as big as a three-room house. It was clean from much use over the years. Not everyone who lived in the house below had shared the same religious faith. The one who used this cave and the one who read the Bible were different people.

The liquor still in the cave had not been used in years, but it was all there. Although the cave was made by nature, it had been developed by man. The stream of water that I had crossed had its origin here. The stove used by the bootlegger was vented into a large crack in the walls of the cave. I would have to examine this to know how much smoke could be seen from the outside.

This was the perfect hideaway. From behind the rock I commanded a view of the valley and the house, but I could not be seen. The cave was isolated, dry, warm, and there was water. No wonder the bootlegger had chosen this place. But for Cindy, June, and me it was a home and an answer to prayer.

Quickly I returned to where the girls waited. It was dangerous, but I could not wait for night. We moved out immediately, heading for the hill and the cave, keeping in the shadow of the trees and the protection of the undergrowth as much as possible. The earth was still wet, which made our movement almost noiseless. We were eager to get to the cave but not careless. I traveled some distance in front of the girls so that if there were trouble, they would have ample opportunity to escape.

With relief and joy we arrived at our cave. For the first time in days we felt a temporary sense of safety. We had a warm, dry, and concealed place to live.

The first job was to get the horses unloaded and living quarters arranged. While the girls organized our living area, I led the horses to the pasture near the barn and turned them loose. If they were found, it would be safe to assume that the finders would conclude they had been abandoned on the farm.

We never ventured out during the day. At night, however, I was busy. Dressed in dark clothing, face blackened with charcoal, I began a systematic search of the countryside. My findings were encouraging. The area was filled with animal trails.

The first night I followed a trail that was used by deer. After more than two hours I spotted a ranger station and worked down toward it. Crouched in the bushes on the edge of the yard I couldn't be seen, but I could observe any movement from the ranger station area. Never really relaxing, watching, and listening for any sign of life, I waited. I watched for a long time, before I began creeping very slowly toward the building.

Then I heard it. Immediately I froze to the ground by a bush. There was no telling what unknown danger might be awaiting me. The sound stopped abruptly.

I waited a long time before making any move because

I had to be sure that it was safe to retreat to the bushes. I knew full well that the lives of Cindy and June were connected irrevocably with my own survival.

Retreating into the brush almost as quietly as a cat, I had a clear view of the house and yard. Alert, and peering out cautiously, I waited for hours. There was no movement and the sound did not recur.

I had no choice. The site must be investigated if we were to live in this area. The grounds appeared unused and the building had a vacant look. But what was the noise I had heard?

As one who fears impending annihilation, I moved a step at a time through the night back toward the house. No wild animal ever made an approach more warily than I. Pressing hard against the building, seeking to merge with the surroundings, I waited for sight or sounds of other living creatures. There were none.

The moon had come out full and bright. In the distance I heard the hoot of an owl. Then I heard that sound again. It was a groan that rose and fell softly, and ended in a half choking gasp.

I moved quietly toward the window. Fearful of being seen I flattened against the wall. Protected by the shadows of the house, I arrived at the nearest window undetected. Cautiously, I looked in.

With a jar, I realized that I was looking directly into the face of a man clearly visible in the moonlight. Again I heard the faint groan of suffering in the still air of the night. I could see the lips forming the sounds. Then there was silence. I heard myself breathe. I even fancied that the thump of my heart could be heard.

The man was suffering. The light was dim, but I could see there was no Economic Mark on his hand. I had to know if this was a fellow Christian in need of help. Dropping on my knees I crawled on the soft dead grass to the back door opening into the room where the man lay. Apprehensive but with courage borne of necessity, I went in.

The room was bare save for the man and the small rug upon which he lay. As I moved toward him, I saw him grab his stomach, bring his knees up toward the abdomen, twist his body, stiffen, and then arch his back. He was writhing in torment, suffering beyond his power to keep quiet. His mournful groans made me feel I was on the battlefield again.

As I bent over the man, I guessed him to be about 60. He had thin shoulders with a slender neck and a face that in younger years would have been called delicate. Now that face was emaciated. His repeated groans were followed by gasps for air. This man was dying.

Forgetting my own danger, I walked quickly into an adjoining room, seeking something to help this suffering man. Fortunately, there was no one else in the house. I found water and a towel with which to bathe his face. As I applied the cool water, he grew quiet and his eyes opened. At first, he did not seem to comprehend anything. Then came fear. His dark eyes reflected unfeigned panic. Out of mercy I spoke quickly.

"I'm your friend. How can I help you? What's wrong with you?"

His head rolled to one side. In weakness he was struggling to change positions. I realized then that he was trying to look at my hands. I held them up.

"Sir, there are no marks on my hands. I'm a Christian."

He relaxed. A smile erased the lines of pain from his face for a moment.

"I'm a Christian too," he whispered. "I've been saved at a late hour, but I'm a Christian."

Out of my own fear I interrupted him to ask, "Where

are we? Are there other people near? Who are you? Can I go for help?"

His answer came slowly and weakly as if spoken in the final stages of fatigue.

"I'm Harold Waters. My wife and I lived on a farm nearby. She was caught away in the Rapture. You're in the center of a national forest that covers two counties. There are no families living close by. This is a ranger station but it was abandoned when airplanes came into use for patrolling fires. You'll be safe. The rangers keep some equipment here but they never come around unless there's a fire."

I interrupted, "Mr. Waters, what can I do to help? Where can . . . ?"

He stopped me. "There's nothing you can do. I've had this sickness for a year. I would guess it is appendicitis. Pray for me to die. I really have no right to ask God even for the favor of death. My wife was a Christian. I've been a moonshiner most of my life."

"Then," I interrupted again, "it must be your cave where we're hiding. It's well hidden on a high hill behind a huge rock surrounded by thick trees and brush."

"Yes, it's mine," he answered. "I have lived there since the Rapture, only going to the farm for food until it gave out. There are goats on the farm, but I became too sick and weak to catch them. There's plenty of food in the forest for a healthy man who can go after it. As my sickness made me almost helpless, I ventured out to find food. The rangers keep an emergency supply here."

His words were cut off by the return of the pain. Choking, he gasped for breath and coughed up blood that began to stain his lips. As I wiped it away, I knew that his problem was not appendicitis.

In the soft moonlight his lips were pale and still. As I sat watching him, suddenly he opened his eyes and gave

133

me a long, steady look. A faint smile came upon his lips, his legs twitched for a moment, then he relaxed. He was forever free from his pain.

For a long time I looked at him. I had found a fellow Christian only to watch him die. There was nothing I could have done to ease his pain, but there was a grave to dig and a man to bury. I found plenty of tools, so I went to work. It was still well before dawn when I placed Mr. Waters in the crude grave. There was no marker. Leaves were spread over the spot to hide any signs of a burial.

The thought returned to me that we were people of the night. We walked and talked at night. We were sick and we died at night.

Daylight was fingering the tree tops when I arrived at the cave. The worried girls had a small fire going and breakfast was soon cooking. As we ate, I recounted the night's experience. It was time to rest, but we were never permitted to relax. We divided up the day watch.

The next night was spent scouting the area in which we lived. Escape routes were laid out. Both at night and during the day we tested to see if the smoke from our fire in the cave could be seen from the outside. We were never able to detect it.

As the days passed, I studied the area for miles around our cave until I felt a kinship with it. On the darkest night I could move at a running pace through the trees to the small streams and the creek. I knew where Mr. Waters's goats were to be found. I knew where the animals of the woods lived and the trails that they traveled. I had made this land mine.

It was not unusual for me to sit quietly by the hour and watch the animal trails. My eyes had grown accustomed to the night. Somewhere I had read that the human eye, when accustomed to the dark, could see better at night than many animals of the wild. I now believed that to be so. And I felt another identity with these wild creatures. I, too, was hunted. I, too, had an area to protect as my home.

Now that I had memorized the area, the next step was to teach it to Cindy and June. We took one trail at a time. Over and over we would walk it and then run it. Our endurance improved. Not only was our night sight better, but a sixth sense seemed to evolve. In the dark we could tell when we were approaching trees, rocks, or a turn in the trail. How? I really don't know. Maybe it was a kind of memory. We followed the trails until together or separately we could travel them at a run in the dark. In dark clothing, faces streaked with charcoal, we were invisible. Because of this training, the girls would have a better chance to survive if anything happened to me.

Our next precaution was to hide survival supplies in the event we were forced to escape. We laid out some of the supplies that we had brought with us. In waterproof bags we prepared four survival kits. Each one had a knife, compass, matches, first aid kit, hatchet, large pieces of plastic, fishing line, and fishhooks. We prepared additional bags of clothing and food. Hiding places were chosen along our trails going north, south, east, and west.

Camouflage to look and smell like part of the forest was discussed and practiced. We would rub our bodies and clothing with strong-smelling leaves from cedar or pine trees. In the summer we used honeysuckles. Most of all, we worked on being silent and invisible, so we could travel at night and have no fear of being lost.Shelters miles apart were selected, but we never left signs that anyone had been there. We learned anew the meaning of patience.

Identifying with nature, we were soon able to recognize and know the habits of many of the animals. We saw the slow oppossum climb the tree, and the cottontail rabbit playing in the moonlight. We listened to the flapping sound of the beaver's tail in the distance, and watched the excited deer wave his tail like a white flag. We were learning, and it was not a school for fun. The lessons were for survival because the food supply was low. Most of our reserve had to be left in the coal mine from which we had fled.

During my first visit to the ranger station, I had seen a radio and an old television set. I had made no check, but I assumed that the electricity was still connected to the house, the barn, and the watchtower. Cindy and June were just as eager as I to know what was going on in the outside world. It was agreed one day that just as soon as it was dark I would make a trip to investigate.

Two hours after sunset I arrived at the ranger station. Hidden in the bushes I waited another hour before creeping noiselessly to the house. Then I listened. There were no threatening sights or sounds. It appeared safe to go inside. Now it was to my advantage to be a man of the night. There was no clumsy stumbling in my effort to get into the house and across the room where Mr. Waters had died and then into the rangers' office.

When I turned on the radio, the music came in clearly but I was hungry for news. It was a long 15 minutes before it came on. Twenty-five minutes were given to Dr. Queen, the Food Administrator for the Alliance of the World. So important was Dr. Queen's position that he was introduced by Prince Goldbar himself. It was evident that things were not going well for the Beast and his world. Goldbar made a passionate plea for cooperation against inflation, for a spirit of compassion that would make all men willing to share the world's inadequate food supply, and for the people to understand the necessity for higher taxes.

It was reported that the major duty of Dr. Queen was to distribute equally the world's food and to do it quickly.

In Africa, China, India, Japan, South America, and Russia there was serious famine. Food must be flown in. Further, Dr. Queen was responsible to ration the food. A special food tax was levied to pay the cost of worldwide distribution and to help finance the Alliance of the World's peace army.

Following the introduction of Dr. Queen, there were news reports from around the world. Events were evidently causing Prince Goldbar's government great anxiety. People seemed near rebellion. He needed support for the food tax, and for the necessity of taking food from a nation that was hungry and giving it to another that was starving. The Beast was fighting for his kingdom.

The announcer skillfully painted word pictures of men and women with "bloated stomachs, pipestem arms and legs, and expressions of stuporlike dullness. Too numb from hunger to talk, they search the streets and alleys for food. They fight like animals for any nourishment that is found. Reports of cannibalism are coming in from every part of the world, including England and the United States.

"People have been seen to attack stray dogs, tearing them apart and gnawing at the raw flesh. Storage bins of field corn are being raided, and some seed for next year's crop has been eaten. Pastures with cattle must be guarded day and night. No food supply is safe without police guards who have permission to shoot to kill in order to protect the food."

Following this report some food prices were given. A loaf of bread was $8.00 in India, $6.00 in London, $5.00 in New York. In many restaurants a lunch was $25.00; five years earlier it could have been bought for $1.50.

Just before midnight I was back at the cave, and gave a full report. June's answer was:

137

"Steve, world starvation, rationing, and high prices were all a part of Bible prophecy. The next major event will be plague and death."[1]

1. Rev. 6:8; 18:8.

# 8

# Black Death

*I looked, and behold a pale horse: and his name that sat
on him was Death, and Hell followed with him. And
power was given unto them over the fourth part of the
earth, to kill with sword and with hunger, and with
death, and with the beasts of the earth* (Rev. 6:8).

Secure in our cave with at least one more year of the
Tribulation before us, we settled down to a routine. To
conserve our seriously limited food supply, we were now
setting snares for rabbits, as I had done when I was a boy.
We found a slender tree, tied a piece of fishing line to the
top and made a slip loop in the other end. Then I notched
a stick and drove it into the ground. A second stick was
notched and tied to the top of the tree. The tree was then
bent over until the notches in the two sticks fitted together. The tension made by the bending tree held the
sticks together. But at the slightest jar the tree would jerk
upward and the loop would snare the rabbit. We baited the
snare with tender grass that we found along the creek
where it was sheltered by rocks and leaves.

For any real emergency, we always counted on a reserve of food in the goats on the Harold Waters farm.

I could not help but feel that God had been with us. Why Matt and the others were not permitted to make it to safety, I cannot answer. But for us, conditions were as near perfect as circumstances would permit.

Our routine now included a nightly trip to the ranger station just after dark. Upon our arrival, one of us stayed as a lookout while the other two watched the news report. More and more the evening programs were filled with propaganda. Often Prince Goldbar himself spoke. From the reports we could sense that things were not improving as quickly as he would have liked. Living in isolation as we were, there was no guessing all of the problem, but the propaganda machinery was being tuned up. One thing was sure, the Jews and the Christians were still being blamed for the world's problems.

Our return home was noiseless. No hunted animals ever journeyed more warily. Dark pines filtered out the moonlight, and we were like three ghosts gliding along the path. At times one could not escape the feeling that the forest hid something ugly and monstrous. It was a feeling of unseen dangers, a sinister threat seeping in from the blackness. A silent, endless fear nagged us.

Then out of the darkness one night a masculine voice spoke my name.

"Steve."

For a moment I froze, actually suspended in a walking position. In this moment I heard nothing but my own quick breathing. But before I could move, the voice continued,

"This is Uncle Tim."

Never in all my life had I been so frightened. My fists had clenched into hard balls, and I felt the prickling of fear at the back of my neck. Even when Uncle Tim identified himself, it seemed a long minute before I could answer. The whole forest seemed locked in stillness for that moment. I felt the blood beat in my temples and my heart hammered heavily.

When I answered, my voice was low and my throat dry. The words tumbled out.

"Uncle Tim! Where . . . ? What . . . ? How . . . ?" I realized that I was not making any sense, but by this time he was standing at my side.

"Uncle Tim, how did you find us? Where have you been?"

"Steve," he answered, "what do you say we go into the cave; stir up the fire, and I'll tell you my story."

Since we were no more than 20 steps from the entrance of the cave, we were soon seated around the fire. When we assured him that all was well with us, he told his story.

"When we were moving north, our group walked into an ambush by McKifer and six of his men. Some were killed, some may have escaped, and the others were captured. I was one of those captured by the police, but I was separated from the others. The reason given was that I was a Christian leader. I believe the others were taken to a concentration camp, but I was taken to a county jail. Later I heard them say that I would be sent to an office of the World Peace Bureau for questioning."

"But how did you get out?" June interrupted.

"Do you remember a preacher by the name of Mannaser?" Uncle Tim continued.

"Yes," the three of us answered with one voice.

"His brother is a policeman. Even though he has taken the Economic Mark, he is friendly to the Jews and the Christians. He doesn't believe the propaganda that the Christians and the Jews are causing all of the famine and plagues in the world."

"What plagues?" Cindy asked before June or I could speak.

"Let me start at the first, and I'll bring you up to

date," Uncle Tim answered. "I'd been in jail for a few hours when I heard someone call my name. Lying on a bunk half asleep, I answered with some hesitation. Somehow the voice was familiar, but in this place I couldn't recognize it."

"Tim, this is Joseph Mannaser."

"What?" In a bound I was at the bars.

"There's not much time for talk, Tim," he spoke softly but quickly. "You know if you don't get out of here before day, you're a dead man. I don't know how well you're informed on world events, but people are starving and in some countries plagues have broken out. Some say the plagues are being caused by China's experimentation with germ warfare. Others say that chemicals dumped into the ocean by the United States caused it. All we know for sure is that a third of the Chinese are dead, and the plague is moving into Europe and the United States. The reason it is killing so many is that the bacteria causing the sickness are resistant to any medication. Famine has the people half starved in most of the world; this also makes them easy prey to the plague.

"Here's where you come in, Tim. The Alliance of the World claims they have proof that the Christians and Jews caused the plague, and that they are using the plague as a weapon to overthrow all governments. Legally Christians and Jews are traitors; all are under the sentence of death. And now they are also hated by the common people who think they caused the plague.


"Tim, I'm not a Christian and I never expect to be, but my brother was. I know the character of Christians, and they don't kill people. I'm the one who dropped the bottles at Ray's Crossing.

"It is 3:00 in the morning," Mannaser continued. "And now it's time for you to get out."

142

"But, Joseph," I protested, "what will happen to you?"

"Nothing if in appreciation for letting you go you'll give me a hard lick on the head, take my keys, and get away in my car."

"Joseph, I promise you full cooperation, but may I ask you one question? If you wanted to hide in a government forest, where would you go?"

"That's an easy one, Tim," Mannaser answered. "Do you remember the old Harold Waters farm back in the county north of us?"

"I sure do."

"If you'll go to the house, and then follow the stream until you see a big rock, behind that rock is a cave that Waters used for his liquor still. Tim, that's the best hiding place I know. The only reason I know about it is because his wife reported the still to try to get Waters out of the business."

"One other thing, Joseph, and I'll be on my way. I see a stack of news magazines here in the office. May I take them? Reading material is important when one sits day after day in hiding."

"Help yourself, Tim."

"Thanks, Joseph, and I'll leave your car where it can be found. I don't know how to express my appreciation for all your help to me and the other Christians."

"Here, Tim." He handed me a police club. "Make it a good one. You know I've got a hard head."

Uncle Tim then concluded, "Steve, I just hope I didn't hit him too hard. I threw out the bundle of magazines not many miles from here as I drove by. We can go back after them. I left the police car in the parking lot of an apartment building. It took me many hours to work my way back here even though I know this area from deer hunting days."

By his constant talk I knew that Uncle Tim was deeply interested in his magazines. After he had rested for a day, he and I started back for them.

"Steve, I want to know more about the famine and the plague. You'll remember the Revelation teaches that when the fourth seal is opened, people will die 'with hunger, and with death, and with the beasts of the earth' (Rev. 6:8). This may be that seal."

As usual, we traveled at night, starting at dark. We were camouflaged with blackened faces and dark clothing. It was a full night's journey, and was getting light when we arrived back at our cave. Twice on the trip we heard others moving in the night. They could have been hunters. Uncle Tim felt sure there was illegal hunting caused by the inflationary price of meat. During the trip I had opportunity to bring Uncle Tim up to date on the ranger station, the television set, and the death of Mr. Waters.

For weeks we watched every news report. From the magazines and the reports we began to piece together a composite picture of a severe famine that had moved through the East and was progressing westward.

In China, India, Japan, Israel, and the Arab countries people were eating anything that could be chewed. Reporters told of seeing people eat food that stank with such rot that it could cause sickness and even death. A mother, father, and three adult children were found starved to death. Their bodies had been partially eaten by rats. A magazine picture showed a starving man sitting speechless, dull, and past caring. Bands of starving dogs were shot while attacking the weak.

The starving included not just the illiterate and those who had always been indigent. Many had been prosperous middle class people; but taxes, unfair laws, and court actions had destroyed that class. The concept that all people should share equally regardless of personal effort had produced a society of privileged rich, and those who lived off the taxed income of the middle classes.

Summer would soon be upon us, and this would give our part of the world more food for a while. Even so, the news magazines and television reports gave instructions for cooking grass, roots, wild onions, and anything considered edible. The time given to this was proof that thousands were barely eking out an existence. The question was, What will people do when winter comes?

The United States could feed itself. But for years the government had followed a world policy of "Take from those who have and give to those who have not." The Bible teaching of equal sharing, "Love thy neighbour as thyself," was forgotten for a policy that completely ignored initiative and personal responsibility.

Now that America was a part of the Alliance of the World, the people had no choice. The Economic Mark program required a computer decision on where the food should go. American farmers were so disheartened that they no longer tried to raise an abundance. America suffered while ships took food from her shores. Multitudes of wretched human scarecrows watched the ships loaded with food leave the harbors of the United States. Stones were thrown, and court controlled police answered with gunfire. The crowds fell back, but some ragged skeletons were left dead.

Bands of starving people marched on government buildings and warehouses—any place that food could be found. Armed guards stood at the doors of all restaurants, food stores, and shopping centers. These famishing men could become wolf packs at any time. Now they were numbed and bewildered, but who knows? Tomorrow this confusion may be succeeded by anger, hate, and panic. The kind of fear and terror that causes animals to stampede can also strike men.

145

Food prices had doubled in 60 days. Even people with some money saved and with jobs were hungry. They could not pay the high prices. The Alliance of the World alone reaped the profits.

Even in the United States men and women were collapsing in the streets, and while standing in relief lines. Begging for food was common. And now, as if starvation were not enough, the new horror of plague threatened the world.

History should have warned the nations. Medical authorities had written, "After famine comes plague." But the scientists had been ignored. The pestilence struck the East with a savagery unknown to historians. It struck suddenly on a gigantic scale ravaging China, India, and neighboring nations simultaneously.

From all over the world there were rumors about the origin of the plague. There was one that seemed very reasonable. In an Eastern country intense experimentation had been in progress to develop bubonic plague bacteria that would be resistant to all known drugs. The experiment included shooting rockets loaded with the germs into space and bringing them back to earth to determine if the bacteria were still active and contagious. Something went wrong, or there was sabotage. A rocket exploded, and now the epidemics were raging throughout the East and moving rapidly into the Western nations. "At the present there is no known cure or preventative," wrote one doctor from the World Health Center.

"Uncle Tim," I said, "we've noticed smoke from distant campfires for several days. Do you think these are made by people fleeing the famine and the plague?"

"Steve, in my mind there's no doubt of this. It's my guess that by the end of summer the forests will be hunted out, and the countryside will be filled with people as long as there is any food to be found. We'd better stockpile all the food we can."

I told Uncle Tim about Mr. Waters's goats. Immediately he knew what to do. We would smoke-cure all the meat we could. The girls could search the orchards and dry apples.

Weeks passed quickly as we smoked meat, dried apples, dug edible roots, and stored them in our cave. We were none too soon. August was hot and dry, and we feared the worst from the people and from the plague.

We were as ready as we could be for "the black death." The screen doors and windows had been taken from the Waters house to screen the entrance of our cave. Food was stored and also protected by screens. The water in the cave met our needs and it was pure.

For weeks we had been too busy to get to the ranger station. Tonight, however, we returned. While still some distance away we saw that the house, yard, and maintenance building were lighted. A ranger's truck was parked in the yard. From the edge of the woods Uncle Tim and I watched two rangers unload supplies. In the stillness their voices were clear.

"John," one of them said, "do you spend all your time reading? We must have brought a truckload of newspapers and magazines."

The one called John answered, "Butler, you know how I enjoy reading. At home I never got to do much." "Also, when we deliver your supplies at Station Six and I get back tomorrow night, I'll be here by myself through August and half of September. Man, if I didn't have things to read, I'd go crazy."

It was an hour before the supplies were unloaded and the rangers were on their way. As soon as they were out of sight, Uncle Tim and I entered the house.

"Uncle Tim, what do you say that we borrow some newspapers and magazines?"

"Why do you think we're here?" he replied, with a twinkle in his eyes.

I could not suppress my laughter. I do believe Uncle Tim would have risked his life to get the news.

"Uncle Tim, I'd feel safer in the cave reading by a candle. Why don't we take them with us and return them by noon tomorrow? Remember the ranger said he would be back tomorrow night. From what he said, he'll be stationed here through the dry season."

"Good enough, Steve. Let's be on our way."

From midnight until morning we read. Again a tragic composite picture of world disaster developed. One writer began with pictures and a description of a large northern city in the United States. Avenues that once were filled with people and cars were now almost empty. A few people hurried along the streets; here and there beggars were seen. Houses appeared to be closed.

It was reported that entire ship crews had taken ill and died, leaving the ships drifting at sea. The illness hit so suddenly that some airplane crews were unable to bring their planes in for a landing. The planes flew on automatic controls until they used up their fuel, and crashed.

People died in their homes, and neighbors did not know until the odor of putrifying bodies told of tragedy. When this happened, large red crosses were painted on the doors, and the bodies were hauled away to be burned.

There were always bands of robbers breaking into houses of the deceased. Those who dared enter the contaminated houses came away with jewels and other valuables. There was little effort to stop them.

The later magazines pictured more and more houses marked with the death crosses. The expressions on the faces of the people showed that they lived in fear. When one walked down the street, he watched as if he were afraid of being touched. The pictures never showed people gathered in little circles, or huddled together as usually happens when they are afraid. This sinister monster drove families apart. Each person endeavored to draw farther and farther from others, back into his own corner of the world. But there was no place to hide. How do people fight the unseen and the unknown? Such persons fight not with the plague but with fear itself.

In each succeeding publication the numbers dying from the plague grew. Now schools, businesses, and all public gatherings were closed. There was a shortage of street cleaners for cities, and the urban centers were becoming filthy and unlivable. Bodies were left lying on the streets for as much as 24 hours. The odors were nauseating.

The most dreaded feature of the disease was its contagion. People forced by circumstances to get out on the street crossed the road to keep from greeting a neighbor. All were warned not to touch the sick or their clothing, for a touch could be the touch of death. Flies or rodents coming in contact with the disease immediately became carriers. A flea that went from a diseased dog to another dog had been known to spread the infection. People were also warned against eating wild animals. These too could be infected.

Bands of abandoned dogs and starving cats were on the streets. Police were ordered to shoot all stray animals. There were to be no exceptions. Men dressed in white suits, gloves, and masks patrolled the streets, picking up the dead people and animals together. These were burned in furnaces or in huge bonfires.

The latest magazine we had told of people fleeing against the order of the government. Roads were barricaded, but still people traveled. Some had a destination, but others were just hurrying away. By cars, trucks, bicycles, or on foot, people fled the silent killer that stalked them.

"Uncle Tim," I remarked at the end of my reading, "People are already fleeing into the country, and it's only a matter of time before they'll be this deep in the woods in large numbers. A few are scattered through the area now."

"Not only will the people be here, Steve, but the plague will come with them. It would be wise for all of us to agree now that we will not touch any of the animals we see. All of our drinking water should be boiled. We should be very careful about even leaving the cave until cold weather returns."

"Why don't we take the magazines back to the ranger station now? If I had known the plague was this bad, I would never have touched them."

"That's a good idea, Steve."

We reached the ranger station just before 12:00, but the rangers and their truck were already there. In fact, they were in the process of loading a few things on it.

"I'll tell you what, John," ranger Butler called out, "I'm not staying here with the forest full of sick and dying people. I'm going to my family."

"Same here, Butler," came the answer from the house. "In fact, I'll be with you in two minutes."

With a feeling of relief, we watched them go. But there was also something threatening in the words, "I'm not staying here with the forest full of sick and dying people."

We took the magazines and papers into the house and were walking out the door when Uncle Tim stopped me.

"Steve, don't you think we should search for all the insect spray, mosquito netting, and rat poison that may be here?"

"I get the idea, Uncle Tim, and I know just where they keep those supplies."

150

It was our good fortune. Most of the new supplies that they had brought were left behind. We left loaded with the very items that might save our lives.

Fear and hurrying can be dangerous because one becomes careless. As we walked, my mind was oppressed by a sense of impending calamity. The forest seemed more threatening than usual. I clearly saw the shadow of the black death casting its darkness over Cindy, June, Uncle Tim, and myself.

Then we heard something. First, it was a far-off, faint sob, so lonely and pain-laden that Uncle Tim and I were shocked into stillness. This was followed by horrible screaming, coughing, and cursing. The shrieks and curses were as loud as a dying man could make.

We walked quickly to our right. Even at a distance, we saw the agony caused by the plague. One man was dead. Pain disfigured the face of the other. His chest expanded convulsively. The opened mouth tried to engulf great breaths of air. The sound was like a wheezing, worn-out bellows. Suddenly he opened his eyes, gave us a long steady look and spoke slowly, "Don't let us lie here after we're dead. Burn us."

Then the dying man began to revile.

"I curse You, God. Would that You were a man so I could choke You. If I could lay my hands on You, I'd tear you to pieces. Christians are fools. You don't deliver from sickness or from suffering. I curse You, God."

The Economic Mark showed clearly on his hand. He had sold out to Satan but was cursing God for his predicament.

How repulsive these people looked from internal bleeding. Vomited blood blackened their faces. Already there was the smell of decomposing bodies. The man shivered and kicked spasmodically for a second as his whole body shook violently. Then he was still.

We had no choice. For our own safety, the bodies had to be burned. As Uncle Tim cleared an area around them to prevent the fire from spreading, I returned to the ranger station for fuel oil. By throwing the oil and pieces of wood on the bodies, we were able to soak and cover them without approaching too close. We threw a match on the wood and left on the run.

For a few days, Uncle Tim and I stayed in the cave. The need, however, to know what was going on in the world was too much for us. When night came, we returned to the ranger station. The reports let us know that the government was in an all-out attack on the plague. The National Guard had been called out. Travel was forbidden. Patrols were ordered to arrest anyone on the streets who did not have a pass.

Emergency laws made it mandatory for each family to report to the district warden if any member became ill with the plague. If anyone entered a house where the plague existed, he could not leave. Where the plague developed, the house was marked with the death cross. Plastic bags had been delivered to every marked house, dead bodies were placed in the sealed bags and placed on the street to be picked up like trash.

It was obvious that science and government had two hopes. It was known that the disease could not tolerate cold weather. They therefore hoped to isolate the disease and hold on until winter. Meanwhile the scientists were making an all-out effort to break through to a cure or to find some preventive medicine.

From the news reports, it became obvious that the laws against groups meeting were not being obeyed. Many evaded the quarantine to abandon themselves to carnal lust as if they believed the maxim, Live and be merry for tomorrow we die. Our culture preceding the Rapture had taught that lust was the highest good. Maturity and sexual freedom were synonymous. Free minds were never to consider any sexual act as sinful as long as two adults consented.

Many of the people were being led in their degradation by the ministers of the Tribulation. They were supposedly ministering to the people by television since the churches were not open because of the plague. On Sunday night Uncle Tim and I watched a telecast by one of the ministers.

His subject was "Love." For him love was lust. He went so far as to say that, although he was a follower of the Prince of This World, even Christians had to agree with him, because Christ's favorite girl friend was a harlot, Mary Magdalene.

It was evident from this speaker that the leaders of the Tribulation churches—bishops, ministers, and lay leaders —were living immoral lives. They glorified Lot and the city of Sodom. Again they distorted the Scriptures to prove their point. The minister portrayed Lot as a participant in Sodom's sins, living there in incest with his daughters. "Yet," he said, "the Christian Bible pictures him as a 'righteous man.'" The minister did not bother to point out what the New Testament teaches, that their sins "vexed his righteous soul from day to day," (2 Pet. 2:8).

With the passing of the middle class, their respectability which had been a preserving influence in society had vanished. All ages and cultural groups were abandoning themselves to carnal lusts—and considered their conduct to be righteous. The Tribulation ministers went so far as to say that the Christians' Bible taught that God made man, and, therefore, that God approved all of man's acts. They twisted the Bible to prove it: "And God saw every thing that he had made, and, behold, it was very good" (Gen. 1:31). They did not bother to speak of the Fall, and the resulting infection of sin.

153

In the name of the church, lewd and drunken revelries were held with ministers leading the members into sin. They laughed, danced, and blasphemed Almighty God in their cities of death. Many of them would soon be swollen corpses but now they blissfully followed the Prince of This World.

Pre-Rapture teachers were in error when they taught that satanic power would be so strong during the Tribulation that there would be no natural feelings and emotions. Those of us in the Tribulation were still human with all the needs and feeling of humans. We loved, hurt, experienced fear and sorrow.

We feared this hideous plague—the most widespread and fatal that the world had ever known. The black bloodstains upon the body, especially around the mouth and eyes, were its trademarks. People were so fearful of the plague that some mothers forsook families, and adult children forsook their aged parents.

On the other hand, there were mothers who served sick families until all had died, and the stricken mothers were left alone. Reporters told of hearing frightened cries coming from closed houses with death marks upon the door. Then the cries faded. They knew what had happened, but they could not know the anguish of the one who died alone.

Other reporters told of seeing family members illegally leaving their quarantined houses and running after the death trucks. They sobbed and asked to die with their loved ones.

One telecast showed pictures and gave in detail the story of a newly married couple. They had been married only two days when the young husband died with the plague. Members of the family placed his body in a plastic bag and left it on the street, but the bride would not leave him. I will let the announcer tell his story.

"I reported the burning of a hotel; I saw people jump from the blazing building. I was in Viet Nam, and I saw young men die, but I have never seen anything like this plague.

"Today I saw a young girl in her wedding dress follow the death truck down the street. Her cries began in a low moan, rose to a high wail, and ended in a shriek. It was the cry of one who has lost all hope."

The news program closed showing the girl still running after the death truck, seeking a love that could never be found.

Historians have reported that some dictators when in trouble have maneuvered their countries into war to turn the minds of the people away from their despair. Prince Goldbar needed such a diversion. He found a scapegoat in the Jews and the Christians. Both had been persecuted before, but now the attack was on the Bible and the teaching of the Millennial Kingdom. The government of the Alliance had already declared Jews and Christians guilty of treason. Now anyone found with a Bible was also guilty. God's Book was declared a book of treason.

To prove the Bible to be a plot against world government, the Scriptures were quoted in government propaganda. "And in the days of these kings shall the God of heaven set up a kingdom, which shall never be destroyed: and the kingdom shall not be left to other people, but it shall break in pieces and consume all these kingdoms, and it shall stand forever."[1]

"This," the propaganda stated, "is treason. How will the Jews and the Christians bring about such a kingdom? The answer is obvious. They have conspired to exterminate the world by the plague. They have contaminated water and food supplies."

---

1. Dan. 2:44.

As one, the people rose up in renewed hate against Jews and Christians. They sought out the hiding places of these hunted people. For anyone accused, even if they carried the Mark of the Beast, there was no hope of justice. They were mocked, robbed, and persecuted. Sermons were preached against them in the churches. Jewish physicians who had served people faithfully were ferreted out of their hiding places and killed.

Mobs broke into the homes of the accused in hope of finding riches. When they had taken everything they wanted, the accused were stripped of their clothing, watches, and jewelry. They were then locked in their houses, and the houses set on fire. For a short time the cries and prayers could be heard above the roar of the fire, but one by one they were silenced by the smoke and flames. The ashes of fathers, mothers, and adult children —both Jews and Christians—became intermingled and their souls went out to meet God together.

Crippled people in wheelchairs were seen shoved into the fires. Old people on crutches were sent stumbling into the flames. Young couples hand in hand walked into the burning buildings. Mature couples embracing for support went forward to die together, but they did not reject their God. Some, too sick and weak from starvation to walk, were thrown into burning buildings. Others were beaten so mercilessly that they dragged themselves away and staggered into the fire, but they did not bow to the Beast.

The more the Jews and the Christians refused the Economic Mark and died, the more they were hated by the government of the Alliance. From the television pictures the eyes of the martyrs seemed fixed on another world; I was sure that their ears heard a voice other than the voice of the mobs.

Not only were Jews and Christians killed. Grudges between persons loyal to the Prince were settled by accusing one another of being secret and disguised Christians. Greed caused brother to accuse brother, and neighbor to destroy neighbor.

No truer words were ever written than that "they should kill one another" (Rev. 6:4).

# 9

# Shaking Earth
# and Dying Saints

*I beheld when he had opened the sixth seal, and, lo,
there was a great earthquake* (Rev. 6:12).

In the late afternoon Uncle Tim and I left Cindy
and June at the cave and started for the ranger station.
A cold wind was blowing and a freeze was in the making.
This was good. The plague had been on the decrease for
weeks, but the Health Department had predicted that a
few days of freezing weather would be necessary to end the
danger.

"Uncle Tim," I spoke with an optimistic voice, "I'll
be glad to see an end to the plague. It's true there've
been some advantages. McKifer and his men have let up
on their hunt for Christians, and the ranger station has
been ours to hear the news each night. But to tell the truth,
I've been afraid."

"Steve," Uncle Tim replied with a trace of a smile,
"you don't think that you've had a monopoly on fear, do
you? All sane men fear. Especially when it's estimated
that one fourth of the world's population have died from

the famine and the plague. And no one will ever know how many Christians have been killed because they were accused of starting this plague."

"Uncle Tim, . . ."—I never completed my statement. I don't even recall what I intended to say. I do remember that we were about halfway between the cave and the ranger station when the earth began to shake. Who can describe the earthquake and the fires and floods that followed?

The first hint of trouble was an awful rumbling like a distant train or a jet plane. It came from the bowels of the earth and grew into a deafening roar.

Uncle Tim and I were flung violently to the ground, which was buckling and breaking up all about us. The shaking of the earth was growing steadily stronger. The trees seemed to be leaping and dancing in the late evening light. Then they began snapping, popping, and breaking. The rumbling earth sounded as if it were straining to hold together and prevent its bowels from spewing destruction upon the land.

It is unbelievable, but I saw waves of earth like waves of water flowing toward me. The very ground began to pitch and beat me with its fists of dirt. As the earth hammered at me, the dust was choking.

I suddenly felt small and alone. My world was shaking as if in the agonies of her death struggle. I kept trying to see Uncle Tim, but in the violent movement and the dusty, suffocating air, I couldn't find him.

But what I saw! The earth cracked open to form a gaping mouth that snapped closed again after swallowing trees as tall as a two-story building. A hill shuddered, sagged in the center and began filling with swirling water to become a muddy lake. The churning, whiplashing earth seemed determined to break every tree, swallow every hill, and destroy all life.

Where was Uncle Tim? What was happening to Cindy and June? These thoughts raced through my mind, and I tried to act on my thoughts. I tried to stand, but I couldn't even crawl. The fearful forces of energy within were twisting, straining, and beating at the crust of the earth. It was much later before I knew that the earthquake was worldwide. Now I only knew that Uncle Tim was somewhere near me if the earth had not swallowed him. Cindy and June might be buried alive in the cave. How helpless! If I could only get to my feet! Then it was over just as suddenly as it had started.

I scrambled up looking for Uncle Tim. Not far away he was struggling out from a pile of loose rock and dirt. Completely covered with dust, the only part of him that I could see was his eyes and mouth. He stood up, spitting dust and talking all the same time.

"Come on, Steve, the girls need us."

We ran as through a battleground. Trails were gone. Trees blocked our path, and we had to watch for sinkholes and cracks in the earth. It was a world that I had never seen before. I prayed as we ran.

"O God, please let them be alive! Please, O God, let them live!"

It was a prayer born of fear—fear like ice crawling through one's veins and chilling his whole body. The air was cold, but I was covered with sweat as we approached our home.

There was no longer a cave. Even the hill and the big rock were gone. Atomic bombs could never have dug up the ground as the earthquake had.

As we climbed down over rocks and broken earth, a new fear invaded my mind. Would water soon be filling this hollow, making a new lake? I had read that Reelfoot Lake in Tennessee was formed by an earthquake, and I knew that Black Creek was nearby. What about the spring that supplied water to the cave? There was every evidence that this was an area of abundant underground water.

"Cindy! June!" I called and prayed, scrambling through this nightmare, stumbling, falling over debris, and choking on the dust. I could not even locate the cave area for sure.

"Only demons could cause this, Uncle Tim," I spoke in much bitterness.

"June! Cindy!" Uncle Tim was calling from my right.

"Steve! Over here! Please hurry!" It was Cindy's voice from the dust and blackness.

It seemed that I fell a dozen times, and I am sure that Uncle Tim did, too, before we finally reached Cindy. She was sitting on the ground holding June's head on her lap. June's legs were caught under a large boulder. Fortunately for June, she was unconscious.

Uncle Tim and I covered June with our coats and began to search for poles to remove the rock. How futile it seemed, searching in the darkness of a strange world for poles strong enough to pry up a huge boulder.

"Here are some small hickory trees," Uncle Tim called.

Within a few minutes we had two strong poles which we used as levers to lift the rock. As we lifted, Cindy carefully pulled the still unconscious June free.

We soon had a fire going, and still using our coats as covers we made June as comfortable as possible.

"Now what do we do, Uncle Tim?" I asked.

Without answering Uncle Tim turned to Cindy. "How bad is she?"

"I don't know. It all happened so suddenly. We heard a noise like thunder in the ground, and we ran to the cave entrance. The next thing I knew, the ground was heaving so that I couldn't stand. I fell flat on the earth outside the cave. I felt the ground give way under me like

161

a falling elevator. It was totally dark. At first I feared that we'd be buried alive. We were flung about with tons of dust and rock and trees. I tried to stand but couldn't. I shouted for June, but no answer. When the shaking lessened to a tremor I began to search for her. It was then that I realized the hill had literally fallen down. The dust was so thick I couldn't see. How I prayed that God would help me find June. I actually stumbled over her."

"Cindy, you and Uncle Tim stay with June. Keep her warm, and I'll try to find water." It took me nearly two hours to make what should have been a 30-minute trip, but I was successful.

Nature plays tricks. Some are bad and some are good. The good for us was to find the Waters house still standing. The small stream by the house was still flowing. I returned with a bucket of water and several old blankets that were in the house. June was still unconscious and moaning pitifully. By the light of the fire I saw faint signs of bloodstains on her mouth as we bathed away the dirt. her body twitched, her face was too pale, and the lips trembled a little.

I called softly, "June, June."

To my utter surprise her eyes opened. "Yes, Matt."

I took her hand. "June, how do you feel?" Then I realized that she was looking past me.

"Matt, I'm hurting so much, but I'm coming to you," June whispered softly. Not one of us spoke.

"Oh, Matt, you have the baby with you! Matt, I've missed you so much. I've tried hard to be brave, but I'm so tired."

A smile lit up her face. Her eyes sparkled, then closed.

I started to speak, but June opened her eyes again.

"Dad, Dad, you're there, too! Oh, Dad! You, Mother, Matt, and the baby. The baby looks so beautiful. Matt,

162

you look rested, and all of you seem so happy." Her eyes closed, and I thought June was dead.

For a long, long time I just looked at her. Not a tear, not a word. I just looked and remembered. One by one the Christians were falling. How much longer could any of us hold out? We seemed to be fighting not only Prince Goldbar and McKifer, but now the very powers of hell seemed to be directing nature itself in the battle against us.

Suddenly June opened her eyes again. She moved her head slowly and looked directly at the three of us. She gave me a long steady look, smiled and spoke in a whisper,

"Steve, you, Matt, and I have been through a lot of good times and a few hard times together. Hold true to God, Steve. The battle is almost over. Good-bye, Steve. Good-bye, Cindy. God bless you, Uncle Tim."

Again she looked past me. This time she reached out with both arms. "Matt, I'll take the baby now." June was gone.

The moment of death brought sadness, but it also brought faith. Sorrow tore at the heart of each of us. Tears were mixed with the dust on our faces. We felt helpless. There was no clean, new clothing for burial. There were no flowers, no casket, no songs.

We wrapped June in the quilts until day. It was gray dawn when we made a litter from one of the bed covers and two poles. Uncle Tim and I put the body on the litter, covered it with a quilt, and started for the Waters house to find boards to construct a box for burial.

We buried June in a box made of rough lumber placed in a rudely dug grave.

Uncle Tim's prayer was short but meaningful: "O Lord, we commit to the ground the body of our loved one. Receive her spirit into Thy kingdom. Keep and protect those of us left behind until we are called from this battle to the Church Triumphant."

163

We were tired, sick in spirit, and destitute of worldly goods. There was, however, no time to feel sorry for ourselves. This was another day. We needed food, shelter, and clothing. We couldn't find the supplies that we had buried for an emergency.

The Waters house was no longer usable. It was old, and now, twisted by the earthquake, it had half fallen in. Moreover, it would be a dangerous place if McKifer started on the rampage again. This would be one of the places he would watch.

The beauty of early sunbeams gilding the few remaining treetops brought some cheer. For a moment I found myself dreaming wistfully of home, the big white farm house, the apple trees, and lazy summer days. For these few moments I had a feeling of peace and security that belied all reality.

But truth returned as I looked again at a new-made grave. Now there were only three of us left in a devastated world. My lips did not move, but inwardly I was whispering, "Home, Home, Home."

The hopelessness of our condition seemed to ooze up from the destruction of the earthquake. It was like some evil spirit infiltrating my bowels with fear, creeping into my mind with numbness. I felt the doom about me, clutch at me, mocking me. I knew that fierce powers of evil lurked near wanting all of us to die. Again I sought mature wisdom.

"Uncle Tim, what do we do now? We have no food, no shelter, no extra clothing. If Antichrist's police lose their fear of the plague, this place will be watched constantly."

"Steve," he replied, "I've been thinking about it. We can't stay here. We're about 50 miles from home, though our protective route through the woods will be longer. I think we should try for home."

Cindy then spoke up.

"I slept very little last night; I prayed most of the time. I believe God would have us go back home."

We decided to start immediately after breakfast. But what breakfast? That was the thought in my mind and, I suppose, in the minds of the others.

Near the Waters house we found an old cellar with 21 withered potatoes that in our more affluent days we would have thrown away. Today, however, these shriveled potatoes were more precious than money. Fortunately, we still had matches. Soon three potatoes were baking in the ashes of a warm fire and, still fearing the plague, we had drinking water boiling in the bucket.

An hour later, with Uncle Tim in the lead and our remaining 18 potatoes wrapped in the blankets, we were on our way.

I tried to fix the picture in my mind, for I felt sure that I would never see the earth like this again. The land and the trees were broken in every direction. Rocks broken from beds of 10,000 years lay scattered in the valley. Streams of water trapped by landslides were becoming lakes. Later some of these would break and cause flooding. Uprooted trees lay on the ground with limbs reaching out as if pleading for help. Some had sunk in quicksand with only the tops still visible. Others, half swallowed by the earth, appeared to have been cut away and then to have been replanted. As I walked by, I touched the tops of trees that had stood 40 feet in the air.

The earth had broken and buckled both on the mountains and in the valleys. No area had escaped without scars. Great craters lay open around us. Rocks as big as houses were stacked on each other as if they had been climbing to escape the palsied earth.

There were birds, but no songs. They seemed shocked and only sat and looked. I walked past a female fox killed by a fallen rock. Her pup stood guard over its dead parent. The pup, too, would soon be dead from starvation.

Only small pines and scrub oaks were still numerous. They had been able to bend and give with the shaking earth because their limbs were short and their tops were not heavy.

The hoplessness of our present circumstances and the peril of the future plunged me into intense gloom. For the first time I felt there was no use trying to survive the last months of the Tribulation. But action lifted me from despair.

Uncle Tim led the way. He was the only one of us who could find the way home. Cindy followed him and I came last.


As we walked, I recalled Cindy standing by the fire in our coal-mine home—her dark eyes, her full red lips, her straight white teeth, her long, lustrous black hair. She had been all that a cultured lady should be, graceful and beautiful. In her voice had been the sound of a smile. Even with the loss of her family, she had remained exuberant with health and spirit. But the Tribulation did not cultivate nor preserve beauty.

Now I saw her as she appeared after these years in the forest. She had changed so much, especially in the last year. Her hair was bleached and her face was chapped by the wind. There were no lotions, shampoos, or bath oils for her to use. Her hands were rough with fingernails broken and unkempt. Not even a nail file was available. Her walk was now masculine, with long, firm steps. No one could live as we had—climbing hills, fording streams, struggling through forests—and remain feminine. The dainty lady had been lost in the long, hard struggle to survive. Her face looked old and tired with only a few hints of youth and buoyancy. Her expression was drawn and the firm line of her mouth suggested extreme effort to keep going. How brave! Dear, dear Cindy!

I kept telling myself that I was too tired to grapple logically with the facts of the Tribulation. I was not sick or hurt. I was simply weary. We had tramped too many days and too many miles since we had first started to live out the seven years of the Tribulation. One thought kept tormenting my unutterably weary mind: there are worse horrors to come.

I was brought back to the realities of survival by Uncle Tim calling my name.

"Steve, it will soon be noon. We'd better take a break, bake some more potatoes and boil some water. We won't stop again until dark."

We rested beside a fallen oak tree. The sun was warm, and the tree sheltered us from the cold wind. Sleep was making its demands, and I said, "Uncle Tim, why bother to boil the water or cook the potatoes. Let's eat them cold. I believe sleep is more important. We need rest."

"The earthquake," he rejoined, "buried many of the victims of the plague. This could be bad as well as good. If one of them has fallen near our water source, we could drink contaminated water."

His voice was tired and understanding but firm. So I built a fire. The potatoes and water helped. I tried again to get some time to rest.

"Uncle Tim, why don't we rest now and travel at night. Isn't it dangerous for us to be exposed in the day-light?"

"Yes, it's dangerous," he replied. "We may be seen and arrested, but the danger of night travel is greater. There is quicksand all around us. You've noticed that we have dodged all the wet spots. Also, there are many cracks in the earth where we could trip and break a leg. We've been trying to follow a trail although it disappears at times under landslides and debris. We'd never make it at night."

All through the afternoon we walked. Each hour we saw new areas of ruptured land or a forest of trees scoured from the hills by sliding rocks. Great landslides of earth blocked our progress. We were forced to move slowly when we needed to travel fast. Fearful of the gaping fissures that blocked our way, the approaching night did not help our peace of mind.

All day we had struggled against the broken earth. Now we walked with hanging heads. Cindy showed increasing weariness with each added hour. Uncle Tim's face was unshaven and hollow with bags of fatigue beneath his eyes. We were utterly worn out. When Uncle Tim called us to halt for the night, my body felt like a mass of cuts and bruises. We had walked all day with few words, saving our breath for the journey. Now we sat by our campfire, exhausted, with little hope for the future.

We ate two potatoes each, drank our hot water, prayed together, and each one rolled up in two blankets for the night. I should have slept the sleep of the exhausted, but sleep would not come. In the distance I heard the howl of a dog.

Intense fatigue rendered clear thinking impossible, but again I really felt the hopelessness of the times that I was living through. I had little control of my thoughts as I relived my childhood, the days at the university, and the first years of the Tribulation when our group of Christians had been together. Now only three of us were left.

I again recalled the Cindy of the early Tribulation: her healthy erectness, her physical vitality, her courage, her faith. Her appearance showed the ravages of the strain, but there was no erosion of her courage and faith. Never once had she complained of hardships. More than once her expressions of faith had been a source of strength. How I wished that I could have spared her these trying days. And what lay ahead? That was my personal torment.

Then I thought of Uncle Tim. His face was covered with a scraggly beard, his clothing was ragged, his shoes were worn, and his eyes dull. I did not look any better. And things would get worse. Even though we had lived in a coal mine, we had been well supplied with food, clothing, and shelter. But now we had six blankets, a few matches, and nine potatoes.

Haunting pictures of June dying, Matt, Rob, and Ben being killed, McKifer pursuing us with dogs, the Dobbs family being murdered—all of these streamed through my mind. But sometime during the night unconsciousness came, and I slept the sleep of the exhausted.

Day came cold and gray. The sun was up, but frost still covered the earth. Cindy and Uncle Tim were already sitting close to the fire. I did my best to bring a little life and optimism into my voice as I said,

"Good morning, Cindy, Uncle Tim."

Cindy replied, "And good morning to you, Steve. Come on over for breakfast. Our speciality for today is baked potatoes, hot water, and cold weather."

We were all slightly bewildered by the situation; but we laughed, a deep uninhibited laugh, the kind that reaches down inside and brings out buried fears, washes the soul, frees it from bondage, and leaves hope.

Cindy! I thought. Wonderful, brave Cindy! As tired as any of us but still full of courage. As I looked at her by the fire, I saw a glow of daring in her eyes, an expression of fierce defiance and intense determination. Here was a woman who would survive the Tribulation.

"Steve," Uncle Tim's voice was calm and matter of fact. "Cindy and I feel that we should force our march today. We'll take some extra time to go by farmhouses and look for food."

"But what if we're caught?" I protested.

"Even so, there is no choice. We have only six potatoes left. We must have food. It will be several days before we can reach home."

It is amazing what a little food and hot water can do for a person. In 20 minutes we were on our way, spirits improved with the food and dreaming of home.

For four more days we traveled, eating our remaining potatoes, some eggs, half frozen fruit, and a few cans of beans that we had found at an abandoned farm. At the end of the fifth day we stood in the edge of the woods back of the old home place.

Even with night closing in, and with the desire to rush unceremoniously toward the house, we held back, hiding and watching. I could feel the familiar earth beneath my feet. Even the sky seemed friendly. We were at home.

However, we all knew the gravity of the situation had not diminished. Not one of us was tempted to shout, We're saved! We were at home, but we were not in the Millennium yet.

The house was still closed and shuttered. The earthquake may have done some damage, but, if so, it could not be seen from where we stood. There were, however, signs of beginning decay. It was weather-stained, but still proud and defiant. We watched and listened for half an hour while it was growing dark and colder.

"Uncle Tim," I said, "you and Cindy stay here. I'm going in to see if it's safe for us to stay there tonight."

"Be careful, Steve. We'll wait here for your report."

Half crouching I moved to the right so that the old tool shed would be between me and the house. I was able to get within 50 feet of the back door without being seen.

Keeping close to the tool shed and hiding in its evening shadow, I listened. After waiting for a long time,

I began to crawl on all fours through the bushes and tall weeds toward the house.

Then I heard it. It was only a slight sound, like the slow opening of a door. I flattened as close to the ground as possible and listened. The back door of the house had opened a few inches. A man's head appeared. In the evening darkness I could not tell who it was, but there was a man. I was frightened, but there was no temptation to panic. I remained hidden in the tall weeds and grass because there was no telling who this person might be or what he might do.

Suddenly I came to full alertness. Something was moving in the grass. It was coming toward me. Then I heard the sniffing of a dog. So sinister was the sound that even in its familiarity it had the authority of doom. My thoughts were, "McKifer's dog!" Even though my heart hammered and a current of fear raced through my body, I was determined to give a good account of myself to McKifer and his dog. I lay so still that I am not sure I was even breathing, hoping and praying that the dog would go away. But on he came.

Suddenly there he was, licking my face—he was my own dog.

"Jack, good old Jack!" I whispered. When we left the mine he had come back home.

When I looked back toward the house, the door had closed again. I crawled back to the tool shed, and then in a crouch I ran back to the woods. Jack did not follow me. Evidently he had found a new master. With a lack of caution I went straight to Cindy and Uncle Tim.

In a moment I had given my report and we made our decision to spend the night where we were. No fire, no food, and no water. We simply wrapped up in our blankets and tried to sleep.

Daylight came dull and gray, and with it, we were on

our way to the coal-mine home. By the time the sun was bright, we were there. The earthquake had completely closed the main entrance, or McKifer had blown it up. We circled to the back entrance. There it was, just as we had left it. Small, and hard to crawl through, but we could make it.

"Uncle Tim, you and Cindy wait outside. I'll light a torch and explore the mine."

"Be careful, Steve." Cindy's voice was serious and concerned.

A little later I was back.

"Uncle Tim, I can't believe it! Miraculously everything is just like we left it! We even have electricity. The cave-in at the front buried the wire, but it didn't break it. The extra supports that we put in kept the tunnel from caving in. We have a home and plenty of supplies. Follow me! The lights are on!"

Cindy came with the eagerness of a child at Christmas. Uncle Tim was quiet and serious. I assumed that he was tired. Home was too good to be true. All of our supplies were still untouched. We had stacks of food.

"Steve, get the gas stove going, and I'll get breakfast."

"Will do, Cindy." My spirit were high.

"I'll get the TV going," Uncle Tim added. "We're in time for the WNAV morning news."

By news time we were well fed, rested, and felt more secure than we had at any time since leaving this hide-away. It was with sincere thanks to God that I sat down to watch the Doug Kelley report.

"Good morning. This is Doug Kelley with your morning news. Today we have a special report on the first worldwide earthquake. Our guest is Dr. Fred Hamby of the Geology Department of State University. It is our hope that his information will help the public understand better what has happened.

172

"Dr. Hamby, here is a picture of a western city that is 95 percent destroyed. I was a reporter in World War II, but I never saw a city so completely devastated. How does the energy of an earthquake compare with that of an atomic bomb?"

"Doug, all of the atomic and hydrogen bombs in the world would not have energy to equal the destructive power that was released on this earth during the quake."

"Here is another picture, Dr. Hamby, of a city hit by earthquake, fire, and flood. The reports are not all in, but from what we know it is believed that one-third of our western states were destroyed; cities in the east were almost annihilated."

"For a long time, Doug, scientists have known that the major earthquake belt is around the Pacific with less dangerous faults along the Mediterranean, Atlantic, and East Africa. The earthquakes in the Pacific area, therefore, were not surprising. However, we know that earthquakes can happen in any part of the earth. There are normally about half a million quakes each year."

"Dr. Hamby, some reports spoke of shock waves that in one night were responsible for the death of millions of people. What are shock waves?"

"An earthquake may originate near the surface of the earth or it may be 300 or 400 miles inside the earth. There are many causes for these shock waves that travel up to 22,000 miles an hour through the earth. They are like the ripples formed when you throw a stone into a pond."

"These pictures show the destruction in the United States, Dr. Hamby, but it is also reported that large parts of Asia were almost totally destroyed. Russia and China will release no reports. Is there any way that people can be prepared for earthquakes?"

"No, they come without warning, and the first shocks

are the most severe. Previously the destruction of earthquakes has been limited to small areas. This is the first time that such devastation has been worldwide."

"Professor, since these earthquakes occurred on more than one continent, would this account for cities in Asia, Europe, Africa, and the United States being submerged by great waves?"

"Yes, when earthquakes occur on the ocean floor, waves are formed that may travel as fast as 500 miles an hour. Moving at this speed, they pile up along shores, causing great damage."

"Dr. Hamby, I've just been notified that our first direct reports are coming in from the West Coast. Thank you for being with us today. We switch now to Lewis Cummins for an on-the-spot account."

"This is Lewis Cummins. I am standing on one of the few hills overlooking what was at one time a great American city. Only a remnant is left. Great clouds of smoke from a thousand fires drape the desolate land. This is a silent city of dazed people. To see the destruction is to feel a black dread creeping into the brain.

"People are groggy. Minds have slipped into troubled blankness. Near me is a ragged man with bruised hands; dirt and tears cover his face. He keeps telling how he dug his family from under the bricks of their fallen home, but they were all dead. When he talks, no one listens because their families are also dead.

"Some sit silently by a small bundle of clothing that by some means they managed to recover from the destruction of their homes. The bundle holds all their worldly possessions.

"In a matter of minutes the city was reduced to rubble. Hundreds of thousands are dead or missing. The cemeteries are not large enough to hold the bodies. After almost a week, many survivors still wander around in a daze. They search for relatives or maybe for a memory that will tie them to a past that was lost in minutes and will never exist again.

"The military are here with food, blood, and medicine, but the real need for this city is a new land and a new hope. The business section is under 10 feet of water, and the suburbs have burned. The city is no more.

"The camera crew and I were returning to the city when the earthquake struck. The highway seemed to leap skyward. Giant sections of concrete piled up as the highway heaved, buckled, and twisted. The car pitched like a wild horse.

"I staggered from the car to face wide cracks in the road that could swallow a house. Cars filled with people were swallowed by fissures that appeared bottomless. I looked into the distance for something reassuring, but snow-capped mountains had shaken loose from beds where they had slept for ages to rain snow and rocks upon us. Signal Hill had erupted into an infero that no earthly power could stop.

"My city was gone, but my most shocking experience was yet to come. I looked for the one thing that would not and could not change: the ocean. What I saw was impossible. The water was gone. The bottom of the bay was bare as far as I could see.

"I screamed to the camera crew, 'Run men! Run for your lives!' I had read of earthquakes that pulled the water out to sea only to send the ocean roaring back with a vengeance.

"When we reached high ground, we looked back to see mountains of white breakers racing toward us. Shock waves from the earthquake were pushing billions of tons of water into the city. Wave after wave surged toward Signal Hill. I saw the water become high tides of fire as burning oil was picked up and carried on the waves. Water and fire hit the power plant to fill the air with brilliant bluish electrical flashes.

"The ocean moved inland for miles. Ships were torn from their moorings. The Queen Mary, anchored in Long Beach, was lifted and washed for more than a mile inland.

"Miles of land with houses and people sank from sight to become the bottom of a new salt water lake. Winds became strong and drove the fires to greater anger. From the earth, deafening roars continued to testify to the agony of a dying planet.

"Only a few people had opportunity to flee for their lives. From a dead city, this is Lewis Cummins returning you to your announcer."

"This is Doug Kelley again, with a special bulletin from the Civil Defense. 'The shock waves have ruptured the depths of the earth as well as the surface. Underground and surface river channels have been changing courses; sinkholes pockmark the land. Do not step on or drive on any damp areas. Again, *Do not step on or drive on any damp areas.* There may be only a few inches of soil with deep water and mud underneath.'

"I would like to personally warn you against the many beds of quicksand. When I was on the West Coast to gather the materials for this report, I saw a car coming toward the foot of the hill where I stood. As it pulled off the road it began to sink. A man and his family made an effort to get out and climb the mountain. They never made it. Four people and the car were quickly submerged in a lake of dirty sand. The cameramen and I ran toward the car to help, but were stopped by a military patrol. A sad-faced officer warned us, 'See the water seeping from the ground ahead? If you go another 30 feet you, too, will be a victim of quicksand.'

"As we turned back, I heard a gurgling sound from

the earth. I felt as one who walked in a land of malignant powers that had been released to wreak terrible vengeance upon mankind.

"This is it for today. The earth has been tortured by every force known: plague, fires, floods, storms, and earthquakes. If there is to be further disaster, it must come from the heavens. This has been Doug Kelley with the . . ."

I turned off the television, too troubled to listen longer. Uncle Tim and Cindy had already turned away.

# 10

## Exploding Sun
## and Suffering Men

*Men were scorched with great heat, and blasphemed the
name of God, which hath power over these plagues: and
they repented not to give him glory* (Rev. 16:9).


All morning the three of us worked at rearranging our
home. My assignment was to check out and refill our gas
lamps. It was too dangerous to work with gas in the close-
ness of a mine so I took a five-gallon can of gas and the
lamps to the entrance.

When my job was done, Uncle Tim and Cindy had
completed their clean up. By noon things were in order and
Cindy had a good meal prepared.

"Uncle Tim, what's wrong? You're troubled about
something. We have so much to be thankful for. If our
hideaway had been discovered, we could have lost everything."

"That's just it, Steve. Things are too perfect. Everything is here. Even the electricity is still on. Couldn't
this be a trap?"

I knew that Uncle Tim could be right. Who had

opened the door at the old home place? Had McKifer been watching for me? Because of my visit to Dr. Smithson he knew that I was a Christian. For his help to me the doctor had been executed.

Suddenly I felt that I had never known a time in my life when I was not hiding. The will to run had left me.

"Uncle Tim, this may be a trap. Someone is at the old home place. They may be watching, but I am just too tired to run. If we ran, where could we go? I vote to take our chances and stay here."

"So do I, Uncle Tim," Cindy agreed. "There is no place to go. We are people without rights, without protection and . . ." Cindy stopped and walked into her room. I heard her crying softly.

"Steve, I think you and Cindy are right. I don't see that we have any choice. But I do believe this is a trap. For instance, who fed your dog? Why did he leave us to go back to the old home place? Someone has fed him regularly. Either a good friend stayed here to protect things, or McKifer has a trap."

I lay back on my bed for a minute, an hour, or hours —what difference did it make? I was conscious only of this terrible dread. What if McKifer came? I was oppressed by the sense of being trapped. One thing for sure, he would never take Cindy without a fight. I knew this, and I was just as sure that Uncle Tim felt the same.

Lying there I dreamed of home, classrooms, summers on the farm, and of friends now raptured or killed. The complete silence of the cave troubled me. My mental pictures of the outside world with its broken trees and wrecked earth added to my dejection and feeling of doom.

For more than six years I had escaped the powers of Antichrist's government, but for what? Matt, June, childhood, and home all seemed unreal. The past seemed to be only a fantasy.

179

"Steve." Uncle Tim's voice was soft, but in my mental state it sounded alarming. "If this is a trap, and if McKifer should come, don't you think we should have an escape plan? Not so much for you and me, but you know the horrors that could be in store for Cindy. It would be much better for her to die here than to be taken by McKifer."

I was immediately up and alert. "Uncle Tim, the best thing would be to make some fire bombs. We have gasoline and bottles; it's a simple matter to turn them into deadly weapons. They taught us how in the military. I could have a half dozen ready in a few minutes."

Only two were finished when I was abruptly brought to a halt. From the entrance of the cave came a low, mocking laugh that was almost a snarl. It was followed by a command: "Come on out, Christians. We've been waiting to welcome any of your friends, but there don't seem to be any more. We're glad to see you." McKifer's voice was full of vicious irony.

Uncle Tim answered before I could. His voice was cold and level.

"We're coming, McKifer." Then he whispered softly, almost gently,

"Steve, bring a fire bomb but stay behind me."


We crawled toward the rear entrance ready to protect Cindy with our lives. We never had the chance; in fact, we never needed it.

The first unnatural event was the distant sound of strong winds and heavy, rumbling thunder, then a crashing roar. These were not the sounds of some violent thunderstorm. They were unearthly—sounds that would strike terror to any man's heart, and they were only the forerunner of others. There was something satanic in the air. Louder and closer came the awesome sounds.

Above the roar and the wild wail of the wind there

was an explosion. The whole fury of the heavens seemed to have turned on the earth.

Simultaneously, a red glow filled the small opening of the mine. I remembered the gasoline that I had left at the entrance, but what had ignited it?

With the red glow came screams from McKifer and his men, the most horrible screaming I had ever heard. Uncle Tim, Cindy, and I huddled close together in utter fear and confusion as we listened to the roar of the wind and the terrifying screams interspersed with vile cursing. What was happening? From a calm morning to howling storms, exploding fiery heavens, and now screaming men.

"Quick, back deeper into the mine," I urged. "This must be an atomic explosion."

We could hear a full storm of violent winds and see through the cave's entrance the red of the burning heavens. There was thunder and lightning. If this were an atomic war, it would be a time of worldwide burning and destruction. One thing I knew: this was more than my can of gasoline which had exploded, even though I could smell it burning.

Above the sound of the wind I heard a long wail, and I saw the form of a man fill the entrance to our mine. Fully conscious of the danger of atomic fall-out, I crawled toward him.

"Get back, Cindy, Uncle Tim! I'm going after him. Don't get close! Get back!"

"Steve! Steve! Come back!" Cindy, too, realized the danger. But I had to save the man if I could.

As I neared the opening to the mine, I could smell the heat. My nostrils flared, and my mouth sucked for oxygen. I was being smothered. Sweat was dripping from my forehead, and I could feel it trickling down my arms.

I distinctly heard three sounds: the violent winds, the

groans of the man in front of me, and my own panting for breath in the heat and smoke.

I reached out for the man, intending to pull him deeper into the mine. But at my first pull, his flesh came loose. It was as if someone had poured scalding water over his body. The face was red and swollen. His hair and eyebrows were gone. He looked as if someone had forced his face into a fire for just a moment. It was horrible and I was turning sick.

I grabbed his arms again and pulled him toward safety. When I released the arms, burned flesh stuck to my hands. I found myself rubbing my palms against the rocks and the dust on the floor of the mine. I vomited.

Panting, sick, and feeling as if I were slowly suffocating, I looked again at the man lying on his back in front of me. His lips did not move. The groaning had ceased.

He was a heavy shouldered and bull necked man with a large round face. For a moment his eyes opened. His gaze was brutal, satanic, and evil. The man was helpless and dying, but the distorted face was so evil that I had a feeling of alarm. The face so horribly burned retained a scowl, and the red eyes were filled with hate. His tongue moved out slowly to wet his black lips.

I thought he was going to speak. It was only for seconds, but it seemed he gazed at me a long time. His lips moved. He cursed. It was only then that I recognized McKifer, so horribly altered in appearance. The fire had changed his face but not his evil nature. In the very grip of death he cursed God and the Christians.

McKifer began to cough. His body shook. His face already badly disfigured was now turning black. His body jerked spasmodically and then stiffened. McKifer was dead.

Only when he spoke, did I realize that Uncle Tim was with me.

"Here, Steve, I believe you need this." He had a blanket with which we covered McKifer's body. I was bathed in sweat, and I knew that deeper in the mine we would find cooler air.

"Uncle Tim, the heat and smoke are choking me. Let's go farther into the mine. We'll bury McKifer later."

Completely fatigued, and nauseated, I crawled into the cool arms of darkness. I found myself wiping my hands which I imagined were still sticky from McKifer's burned flesh. I was still sick from the smell of the charred body that clung to my hands.

I abandoned myself to mental images of despair. I saw miles of black ashes and rivers hot from burning woodlands. I would never again hear a bird sing or see a dog play. My mind pictured the smoke rising from a thousand burning cities.

Suddenly I realized that the mine was dark. The red glow was gone. I thought little of this, because I knew that the fire after an atomic explosion would pass.

We listened as the winds increased with a steady persistence to a vicious roar. The shrieking monster of destruction was now joined by lashing rains. The thunder and exploding lightning continued. Vaguely I became conscious of a change in temperature from the suffocating heat to a black cold.

I dropped into a sleep of weird and wretched dreams. I heard people screaming, I saw them fall on the streets, and collapse in their cars as the heat and fire circled the world. No land or people could escape. Vegetables would never grow again. No home would be lighted by electricity. No water would run from a faucet. Awake or asleep, I saw only doom. I slept the troubled sleep of one conscious of the struggles of fierce powers.

I awoke to find Cindy and Uncle Tim sitting at the

entrance of the mine. Joining them, I fully expected to see a black, burned out world.

"Isn't it dangerous for you two to be sitting in such an exposed position? Radiation can kill, you know."

"That's true, Steve, but there's something strange going on here. If this is an atomic explosion, we are on the extreme outer edges."

"What makes you think so, Uncle Tim?"

"Come over here and look."

I crawled past McKifer's covered body to sit by Cindy. She said,

"Steve, if that had been an atomic blast, it would have knocked out the electricity, burned the trees, and consumed all the combustible things on the ground. But the trees and woods are not burned; they're only scorched. And the lights still burn in my room." Her voice was low and questioning.

I shared Cindy's confusion, but I understood McKifer's death. My can of gas evidently exploded when struck by lightning. I saw some evidence of a greater fire, and the wind was still strong. But obviously, there had not been an atomic holocaust.

I still had another question.

"Uncle Tim, what occasioned such a strange storm?"

Uncle Tim offered the best solution for the moment. "Cindy, why don't you prepare a meal for us? Steve, don't you think we should bury McKifer before we eat?"

"I sure do."


It was easy to find a ready-made grave in the destruction of the earthquake. In a few minutes the burial was completed. How many men were with him and what happened to them we don't know.

"Uncle Tim,"—I was expressing my thoughts more than I was expecting an answer—"what could possibly have happened to so suddenly scorch the earth and then so quickly cause it to turn cold?"

As we crawled into the coal mine, Uncle Tim did not have time to answer because Cindy was calling us.

"Steve, Uncle Tim, come quickly! Our TV still works. It's time for the news. Maybe we will find out what has happened."

"Good evening," the announcer said. "This is Doug Kelley with the latest. Because of the nature of the news, my guest today is Dr. Ford Mann of the Astronomy Department of State University. We rushed him here for an explanation of the strange phenomenon that the world has experienced.

"Dr. Mann, let me start with these questions. Is it possible for the sun to explode? If that should happen, could it affect the whole world?"

"Yes, Doug, the sun could explode. In fact, it is exploding all the time. The man in the street may say the sun is on fire, but it is not ordinary fire as we have on the earth. The sun is really a great hydrogen bomb.

"Think of it like this, Doug. The sun's heat is millions of degrees at its core. This drives the hydrogen gas atoms into wild commotion. The crashing atoms break up with some parts joining to form new atoms of gas called helium. This is the material of the hydrogen bomb. The sun is just that, Doug, a great hydrogen bomb. On the sun 4 million tons of hydrogen are turned into energy each second.

"Our sun is violent, with constant electric winds and storms caused by electrons that are detached from the atoms. Its surface is in a state of tremendous turbulence.

"The sun is a star, and they, too, blow up. However, for one to do so is rare. What I think the world experienced was a prominence on the sun. Imagine a tornado of fiery hydrogen that reaches 100,000 miles above the surface of the sun; or a blast that sends into space a tongue of fire with a temperature of 10,000°.

"Before today, the greatest eruption on the sun took place in 1946. That eruption was so great that it lengthened the day a fraction of a second for as much as a year. When a blow-up happens on the sun, the escaping gas arches back toward the sun and may extend as a loop for a half million miles or more."

"But what happened today, Dr. Mann? Why did the sun scorch so many fields and people? Some persons in exposed places were burned to death."

"Doug, I think the eruption on the sun shot gas like a geyser into space for hundreds of thousands of miles; this gas exploded, hitting the earth with its heat."

"Then why, Dr. Mann, were we suddenly in the dark, and why did it turn so cold?"

"For a long time scientists have studied what we call sunspots. They appear suddenly and may disappear just as suddenly. We can't be sure of their cause. There are those who think Saturn and Jupiter, because of their huge size and slow motion, may be an influence on the sun. We know that in 1951 Jupiter and Saturn were nearly one hundred and eighty degrees apart with Uranus almost exactly midway between, ninety degrees from each. During this time there was excessive magnetic disturbance.

"On the other hand, the largest sunspot known to scientists appeared in April of 1947. Its total area was 6 billion square miles. This means that more than one percent of the sun's surface was involved.

"Doug, imagine a tornado of fire which reaches funnel-shaped into space. As it extends and expands it cools. That area will seem dark compared to the rest of the sun. This is a sunspot.

"What we had today was an explosion that blasted the earth with strong winds and then waves of extreme heat, followed by a burnout. These disturbances first gave us heat and then a few hours of darkness and cold."

"In other words, Dr. Mann, there was a giant eruption that sent sun bolts far enough to scorch the earth. As this gas moved through space it burned out and there was a cooling process that caused cold and darkness."

"That's about it. Now you asked if this phenomenon were worldwide. In all probability it was. These eruptions occurred periodically for several hours. I feel sure that it was worldwide, but conditions were much worse in some places than in others."

"Thank you, Dr. Mann, for this explanation of the explosion on the sun that took place today. But there is one other question. Should we expect further explosions?"

"No Doug, I see no reason to expect further problems at this time."

"Thank you again, Dr. Mann."

"Now to our Washington reporter to find out what is going on in the rest of the world."

"This is Ted Worth with the world news. Today the sun loosed its fury and might on the earth. One-third of the sun's surface was involved in a blow-up with the titanic force of thousands of hydrogen bombs. This caused hurricanes of fire to soar into space and scorch the earth 93 million miles away. From these fire storms came explosions that shot tons of flames for millions of miles into space.

"Many people thought they were experiencing the end of the world. Around the world people are still in a state of panic. The authorities are pleading with them to exercise control.

"Hospitals are filled with burned people. Valleys once green are now brown. Trees stand naked with their foliage burned away. Paint is peeling from blistered houses. This will be a day long remembered in history.

"Washington is stirred by a rumor from Israel that Prince Goldbar has been ordered to leave that country. For the second time he has been accused of desecrating the Temple."

"Uncle Tim, Cindy," I exploded, "Did you hear that? Goldbar has been in Israel, and they've ordered him out of the country."

"We're listening, Steve. But let's hear all of the report." Uncle Tim spoke as one would to an excited child.

"It is rumored here in Washington that the Allied Nations of the United States, England, Canada, and Australia are of the opinion that Goldbar is looking for an excuse to invade the Middle East. He wants their oil. The Allied Nations are on the verge of pulling out of the Alliance of the World, and they have warned Prince Goldbar to stay out of the Middle East. Some believe that Allied troops are already in Israel.

"For a time, it appeared that Israel was standing alone against the world. Now she has some friends. Here in Washington the Allied Nations have taken on the name of 'Young Lions.'[1] It takes courage for anyone to say No to Prince Goldbar.

"This is Ted Worth with your evening news. Good night."

Almost silently we prepared for bed, each lost in his own thoughts. I assumed they thought as I, Events are moving toward the Battle of Armageddon.

Sleep would not come. I closed my eyes the better to experience visions of things ahead: endless suffering, torments by demons, and war.

All night the wind blew. Its roar seemed to establish it as the dominant power on the earth. I laughed to myself. From childhood I remembered the argument be-

---

1. Ezek. 38:13.

tween the sun and the wind as to which was the stronger. They agreed that the one which could make a man remove his coat was the most powerful. I had just experienced such a confrontation. By day the exploding sun was dominant, but now the continuous sound of the cold night wind announced itself as ruler.

Some write of the morning: "Renewal of life, promises of nature, golden light pure and clean," but this day was depressing. There was nothing poetical about it. Morning came cold and wet. The sun could not break through. Rain still fell, and the wind was cold. In the mine, however, we were dry and cozy. The smell of food cooking and coffee boiling was stimulating.

"I can't get the old home place off my mind," I announced at breakfast. "Someone there opened the door. Someone is staying in the house. As soon as breakfast is over, I think I'll walk over. I can go in the back way and no one will see me. Would you two like to go?"

"I surely would. I can't stand to be penned up here all day," Cindy replied.

"Not me," came from Uncle Tim. "It's too cold and it's snowing. Anyway I need to open our entrance wider and build a door. You two go on. I've got work to do."

When we left the mine, the sky was heavily overcast and the strong gusts of wind gave the snow a sharp, cutting edge that bit into our faces. Even so, it was great to be well-fed, have warm clothing, and feel safe. Also, it felt good to be on familiar grounds. With McKifer dead and if Washington were falling out with Goldbar, there was less to fear from the police.

The snow was mixed with sleet, and the ground was covered as we waded across the pastureland. I was surprised as we approached Black Creek to see steam coming from the water. I was even more surprised when I put my hand into the water and found it warm.

"Cindy," I said, "the sun's explosion was much greater than I imagined. This water is warm. But from the temperature of the air and the appearance of the woods, you would think a hard winter had been in progress for months. I suppose the sun's blackout caused this severe cold weather. But let's forget the weather," I said. "We're on our way home."

I cannot remember when my spirits were so light. I really don't know how it happened, but suddenly I realized that Cindy and I were holding hands and singing "Jingle Bells." Maybe it was the snow and Christmaslike weather.

"Come over this way, Cindy," I said. "You can see the house from here." We were at the edge of the woods and the snow was still falling. The pine trees around us were ragged and offered little shelter. Even with the snow and cold, I welcomed again the sight of home.

"Cindy," I whispered, "let's crawl along the fence toward the barn. This will keep us out of sight of the house. From the barn, I can crawl along the fence row that goes by the house. I may be able to look inside."

"Lead the way," was Cindy's challenge.

Keeping the fence row between the house and us, we had no problem arriving at the barn unseen. I was glad to see that the earthquake had done little if any damage to the barn.

We watched the house for a long time. In this white-cushioned world of snow, it looked absolutely normal; lonely and forsaken but nothing unusual. From a distance I heard the motor of a truck grumble its protest against the cold as it rumbled along the road. Still we watched, never really relaxing.

"Cindy, isn't that a little smoke coming from the chimney on the north side of the house?"

Cindy looked carefully, her eyes fixed on the

chimney. "Yes, it is, Steve. It's from a small fire of very dry wood. That kind of fire sends off little smoke."

"I'll tell you what. You wait here. I'm going to crawl closer and look through the window. The fence on the north side is overgrown with grape vines. This will give me good cover."

"Please, Steve, be careful." Her voice was so concerned that I looked at her with surprise.

She was looking at me affectionately. There was no longer the tired, sad look that I had seen as we had walked the trails of hopelessness. Her eyes shone with excitement and concern, but there was a brief flicker of fear.

I could feel my whole spirit and body respond. I wanted to speak and somehow tell Cindy that I cared for her. But a vague sadness stole over me, and I felt hopeless. What could I say to Cindy? What could I promise her?

"Sure, Cindy, I'll be careful," I heard my voice as if it belonged to someone else.

I kept the fence between the house and me. The thick grapevines gave me excellent protection, and I had little trouble making it to within a few feet of the window that I wished to look through.

I was now opposite the room where the fire was burning. From the protection of the vines I peered out cautiously. The window was not completely covered. If I could get to the house, looking in the window would be simple.

Worming my way through the vines and a broken place in the fence, I looked carefully about and then moved cautiously to the window.

There in front of a small fire sat Enoch Snow, one of my first Sunday school teachers. I quickly retreated to the barn and to Cindy.

"Cindy, you'll never believe who's in there! It's Enoch Snow, one of my first Sunday school teachers!"

"Steve, are you sure? Enoch Snow? Why he was one of the church leaders!" Cindy's voice expressed complete unbelief.

"Cindy, he's in there. Sitting where Dad always sat. You can look for yourself. I know it's Enoch Snow."

We were both caught off guard at the sound of a voice.

"Well, well, if it isn't Steve and Cindy." Snow's voice was pleasant. Cindy and I blinked incredulously.

"I suppose you're surprised to see me. I never thought the Rapture would take place and leave me behind, either."

"But Mr. Snow," I stammered. "How did you know I was here? I mean, how did you know to follow me?"

"Your dog, Jack. Just now he became excited. I looked out the window just as you crawled through the fence."

"Come on into your house," Mr. Snow laughingly invited. "It's cold out here." It was with some doubts that Cindy and I followed Snow into the house.

"Sit down. Let me fix you a cup of coffee. Steve, I hope you don't object to my living here. McKifer and his men took over my house. I had heard that no one was living here, so I just made myself at home. It has been my privilege to protect your property from thieves."

"That's all right, Mr. Snow. Dad was your friend. He would have wanted it that way."

I felt a queer prickling under the skin. Something wasn't right. When he brought the coffee, I watched his hand to see if he had the Economic Mark. There was none.

"Steve, I'm sure that you and Cindy have more questions that you'd like to ask. I'll try to save you the embarrassment of asking them.

"My wife and two daughters were raptured away. When I realized what had happened, I repented. God has forgiven my hypocrisy. My home, bank account, and all that I had were taken from me because I was a Christian. If I am found now I'll be killed.

"I heard there were some Christians hiding out in an abandoned coal mine. When they started killing Christians, I, too, hid in one until my food gave out. Then I came here. I've been living here with your dog, Jack, for several months. I'll leave if you wish."

"Oh, no, Mr. Snow, you may stay here."

"No, Steve, you'll need this place. If I stay here, where will you live?"

I evaded his question.

"Mr. Snow, you stay on as long as you wish. You were a good friend to Dad and I believe that it would please him to have you here."

"Thank you, Steve. You know I get lonesome. If there are any other Christians around and if they have meetings, I surely would like to attend them. We could help each other. I once dimly saw a man silhouetted against the night sky near mine Number Two, but I was never able to get close enough to talk."

"We'll be in touch with you Mr. Snow. We don't know about any other Christians than ourselves. Make yourself comfortable."

"Mr. Snow," Cindy spoke thoughtfully. "Aren't you afraid to be so exposed here? What if some of the police should come?"

"Cindy, there's not as much danger now as there was. Following the plague, earthquake, trouble in Israel, and now the sun explosion the police are busy keeping order among the people. There's talk of the Alliance police losing their influence in the United States.

"There are political upheavals in many places. Some nations feel they are not getting their rightful place with the Alliance of the World government. There's so much social and economic discontent in the English-speaking nations that they are threatening revolution. I wish that it would happen. The way Goldbar takes food and manufactured goods from one nation to give to another is not fair. He only does this for political advantage."

"Mr. Snow," I asked out of curiosity, "why do you speak of revolution? Could any nation or combination of nations hope to oppose Goldbar and his government?"

"I can tell you the reason, Steve. Some say that even now there are one or two million revolutionary troops in Israel. These soldiers are mostly from the United States, England, Canada, and Australia. They are being called the 'Young Lions.' Reports have it that Goldbar is moving opposing World Alliance troops into Egypt over the protest of the Egyptian parliament."

"Mr. Snow, you taught a Sunday school class for years. Do you think these movements could be preparation for the Battle of Armageddon?"

"They very well could be, Steve. Things look so bad that we all need to pray for God's help. You know that even with this possible revolution coming, Christians are still condemned people. If we're caught, we'll be killed as enemies of the state."

"We must go now, Mr. Snow, but we will contact you as soon as we can."

"Do that, Steve. But if you will, I'd like for us to pray before you leave."

Enoch Snow's prayer seemed sincere as he asked fervently for God's protection on Cindy and me, and on other Christians who might be in danger.

# 11

# The Sting of Demons

*I saw a star fall from heaven onto the earth: and to*
*him was given the key of the bottomless pit. . . . And*
*there came out of the smoke locusts upon the earth: and*
*to them was given power, as the scorpions of the earth*
*have power* (Rev. 9:1, 3).

We did not head straight to Uncle Tim. We left Mr. Snow and walked north although our coal-mine home lay to the south. We traveled into the woods away from home for half an hour before we began to circle toward the south. I found myself looking back again and again as if fearful of being followed. We talked little and hurried as if being pursued.

Several times we crossed our own footprints made on the trip to the old homeplace. How carefree we had been when going, but how anxious on our return. I was nagged by something that I should know. Vaguely I felt it, but I could not pinpoint it.

The longer we walked the more a solid suspicion grew. Something was wrong, I kept thinking. Enoch Snow is a traitor. It was like a black shadow that hung over me.

I wondered if I were becoming paranoid. When I looked at Cindy, now pink-faced by the cold, I knew that she was puzzled also. Her eyes were grave and her brows knit in deep contemplation.

Arriving at our home, Cindy preceded me into the mine. Before I could follow she was telling Uncle Tim of our experience.

"Uncle Tim, we found Mr. Enoch Snow living in the old home place and . . ."

She did not get to finish.

"Did he see you?" Uncle Tim's question had a tone of alarm.

"Yes," I answered, "he walked in on us at the barn. Man's best friend, my dog, gave us away. How seriously do you take his finding us? We did not tell him about you or where we live."

"Well, I can't be sure. As I remember Enoch Snow, he was about 60, tall and heavy, with cold, black eyes. He was always smiling but his smile never seemed to include his eyes. He was the most vocal leader in the church, but many people never fully trusted him. It is hard to say why. He always put on a good front, but there were a lot of questions about some of his business deals."

Little more was said about Mr. Snow during the evening meal. Even though I was hungry and the food was good, my thoughts were on Snow more than the food. It hurt to know that my carelessness may have gotten all three of us into trouble.

Could it be just a coincidence that Snow had moved to our house? Could it be kindness that made him take care of my dog?

"Uncle Tim, I don't believe we told you that Mr. Snow had some criticism of Goldbar," I said.

Cindy spoke before Uncle Tim could answer, "He even suggested that a revolution may be in the making against him. Steve, I never did see the Economic Mark on his hand, did you?"

"No, Cindy, but I intended to ask you if a person could use any kind of makeup to hide the Mark."

"I'm sure that he could, but I didn't notice anything that looked suspicious."

"Uncle Tim, could this atmosphere of suspicion be the result of almost seven years of fear?"

"Well, one thing for sure, Steve. We must find out where Enoch Snow has really been. What are his connections? Is he a spy for the police?"

"But how can we do that Uncle Tim? We can't go into town to ask questions. What can we do?" Cindy's voice sounded tense.

"Well, I don't know how we can get information, but I don't remember Snow as a person to be trusted. He was a churchman and a faithful one in attendance, but he never lived above suspicion."

"Uncle Tim," I said, "from Mr. Snow's conversation we know he's been snooping around in these areas. He said he was seeking the fellowship of other Christians. We know that McKifer knew about this hideaway. Should we move?"

"I've been thinking just that, Steve, but I hated to suggest it. I don't believe we should spend another night here."

"But where, Uncle Tim?" Cindy's voice was almost pleading. "Where can we go?"

"I'll tell you what. Let's get things packed as fast as we can. We'll camp out if need be until we find a place. I just don't trust Snow."

Cindy and I packed food and clothing while Uncle Tim chose blankets and other survival items. Within 30 minutes we were ready to go.

There was a sense of relief to be out of the mine in the

fresh air and to be on our way into the night. For five or six hours we pushed deeper into the woods. Seven years of such living had surely hardened our bodies. At the beginning of our hiding and running from McKifer, not one of us could have made such a trip with so little rest.

We walked in silence. The snow settled on our caps and shoulders. Somewhere in the distance a train stopped and backed and repeated this at irregular intervals. The snow made the night light and the walking quiet.

By the first signs of dawn we were fatigued and famished. My thoughts were on rest for Cindy. Her thoughts were a secret. Every few minutes Uncle Tim flung a look back along the way we had come.

"Uncle Tim, there's an abandoned mine village."

"That's old Number One, Steve. But we'd better stay in the woods." We moved away from the coal camp back into the trees.

Throughout the gray dawn we continued to move northeast. We needed a daylight hiding place well away from the village and away from any road.

For some time we had followed a route that led us down a gentle slope toward a creek. We were able to cross the shallow waters on rocks. On the other side was a pasture, and in the distance a pile of wood that had been an old farm house. Evidently it had crumpled and fallen during the earthquake. To the right of the house was an unpainted barn that appeared to be in fair condition. Uncle Tim led us toward the barn.

In spite of the cold wind and snow we were sweating from the difficulty of walking with the heavy loads on our backs. Halfway between the woods and the barn it happened.

I was walking with my head down, trying to protect my eyes from the wind so I didn't see it happen. But

I heard a greedy sucking sound and a cry of alarm. It was the first time I had ever heard Cindy scream.

"Steve! Quick! Your belt!" It was Uncle Tim. His voice was urgent but still controlled.

He had stepped into a sinkhole covered by the snow, and was sinking rapidly in dirty bubbling water and mud. It was as if some under-earth vacuum were sucking him down.

Almost in one move I had my belt off and was lying flat on the ground. I threw one end of the belt to Uncle Tim. He was already submerged in mud and water up to his armpits when he caught the end of the belt.

"Cindy, quick! Hold my feet!" I shouted.

As Uncle Tim began to pull on the belt, I was sliding toward him. I saw his face flush and the veins of his neck stand out as he gasped for air in his struggle to pull himself free. The heavy load on his back was pressing him down, and the sucking sound continued from the sinkhole. Then we had a moment of reprieve; Uncle Tim was no longer sinking, but neither were we pulling him free. His feet had apparently found some firm footing.

The snow got into my mouth and eyes as I lay there clutching the belt with a strength born of fear. My hands were getting slippery from the melting snow, as I struggled with all my willpower to think of some new action.

My arms extended out over the sinkhole, but there was no way that I could reach Uncle Tim. Neither could I get sufficient hold on the belt to pull him free. My arms ached. My hands felt numb.

"Steve, listen!" Cindy's voice had a note of despair.

In the snowy silence of the woods, I heard the sound of footfalls. I could not see anyone from where I lay, and it was impossible for me to turn.

"Steve, some men are coming."

Unmindful for a moment of their being friend or foe, I

199

prayed for help. Now I could dimly see men on my right and on my left, and I heard a voice behind me.

"Well, well, Tim Chandler. It surely seems the mighty have fallen." It was Enoch Snow. His voice sounded cynical.

"Mr. Snow," I responded, "how about helping me get Uncle Tim out of here, and we'll talk later."

"Why should I help Tim Chandler? He killed McKifer, one of my best men."

"McKifer, your man?" My response was involuntary.

A low, mocking laugh came from the group.

"That's right. My man. We'll get Tim out, all right. There are some things we need to know from him. Get him out boys."

In a moment Uncle Tim was standing by me. He still had not spoken.

"You Christians," Snow continued, "have been watched from the moment you arrived back in this area. Your coal mine is bugged. We could have arrested you at any time. McKifer got in too big a hurry. My plan was to let you lead us to the other Christians. I got the feeling, however, that Tim had caught on that we were following you and that he was leading us on a wild chase."

I knew then why Uncle Tim had pushed so hard and had looked back so frequently.

Cindy moved close to me.

Uncle Tim spoke for the first time. "We did not kill McKifer. There was a can of gas that blew up when it was struck by lightning during the storm." Uncle Tim's voice was calm and even. It seemed that nothing could rattle him.

Snow's voice was almost a snarl, "You, Tim, and your family. They always tried to run the church. You felt that you were better than me and my family. Now we'll see who's boss."

200

"Mr. Snow," one of the men spoke in a voice filled with vileness. "You have Tim Chandler, the leader of the Christians. You'll get your reward. Let us have the girl as our reward."

The men were grinning and looking at Cindy.

Cindy looked at Uncle Tim and me. We moved between her and the men. They had guns, and could kill us easily. But they would have to do just that. I was praying as I had never prayed in all my life.

"Well, boys, you have worked hard. You do need a reward. Tim, I used to teach a Sunday school class. I remember teaching about God delivering Daniel from the lions and the Hebrew children from the fire. Do you think God can deliver Cindy from my men?" His voice was suggestive, and as evil as it could be. He smirked as he mocked God.

The four men moved toward Cindy, as Uncle Tim and I prepared to die.

Cindy's voice was calm as she spoke. "If one of you gets close to me, I'll jump into the sinkhole."

They gazed brutally at her, a wolfish glare in their eyes like demon-possessed people.

Snow's face was brutish as he spoke. "Tim and Steve will bring us as much dead as alive. I'd like to get some information from them, but we don't have to. We're the only ones who know about them, so there'll be no questions asked if we bring them in dead. Have your way, men."

As Snow spoke, the men had been regarding Cindy greedily. But they never touched her.

Suddenly, all of us froze in positions of alarm. Far away in the early morning silence we heard a strange sound like the faint hum of insects, millions of them. Then the sound rose to a drone of whirring wings. Louder and louder it became!

When I first saw them, they appeared as a vapor and

then as a black cloud covering all of the western sky. Millions and millions of winged creatures were flying toward us. On they came in perfect formation. Never in my life had I seen such swarms of insects. The sound of rustling wings now became a roar. With horror we stared at the cloud of oncoming creatures. No one moved.

When I glanced at Enoch Snow, he was deathly pale. His lips moved, and I heard him whisper, "It's so. O my God! It's so."

The roar was now so loud that one would have had to scream to be heard. The creatures were so thick that it was getting dark. On and on they came. The heavens were filled with them. Thousands were dropping to the ground farther up on the mountain until the snow was covered. The land was black with them. We were experiencing a living deluge.

Millions more were flying over us. Those on the ground came down the hill that we had descended and poured over the creek that we had crossed. They were all around us.

One fell at my feet. At first I thought it was a locust about an inch and a half long, but it was covered with hair and its tail twitched with a long stinger. Then it turned a horrible but intelligent face toward me. The eyes were alive with a demonic glare. If hell had a face, I knew that I was looking at it. The mouth opened to expose sharp and unusually long teeth for such a small creature.

Its eyes moved wildly as if it were looking for something. The tail twitched expectantly as the stinger flicked in and out. Never in my worst nightmares had I dreamed of such a satanic creature. Each appeared to be enclosed in an armor-like breastplate that made it a miniature fortress.

I was aroused from my hypnotic state by a scream that brought me back to a cold and dark world. The creatures were upon us. We were surrounded by an ocean of them.

I looked in the direction from which the scream had come. One of Snow's men reeled in a wide circle, striking at his face and neck as he half fell. He regained his feet and continued to fight at the creatures.

Like a swarm of bees the creatures were covering the men. Now all of them were cursing savagely. Some cries sounded like howls and others like groans. After firing their guns a few times, they flung them away. It was a struggle of a few men against millions of creatures. Everything was frenzied activity; slapping at their faces, clawing at their necks, and beating on their trouser legs. Weird screeching sounds from the creatures were mixed with savage cursing of men in mortal agony.

For the first time, I realized that I had thrown my coat around Cindy in a protective gesture. Uncle Tim stood in front of me with a strange half smile on his face.

"Come this way," his voice was calm. Just that, "Come this way." It was the voice of one who knew what to do.

I started to protest because he was walking directly into the horde of creatures. To my utter surprise they gave ground and flew away from him. Uncle Tim seemed not to fear them. They feared him.

It was obvious that the creatures did not want to give way to Uncle Tim and us. They would fly and dart about us like bats, but they never came close enough to be dangerous.

As he led the way Uncle Tim prayed. "Jesus Christ, Thou art our Savior and Deliverer, and in Thee do we trust. Even though the powers of hell surge about us, in Thee, Jesus our Lord, we find shelter."

Over and over he repeated the prayer. Each time that he called on the name of Jesus the creatures let out a screech as loud as their small size made possible. It was high-pitched and horrible. We held our hands over our ears and walked on. Uncle Tim continued his prayer.

All about us the creatures were winging like vultures waiting to attack. But something kept them back. It was the creatures that hated us and feared us. It was not we who had to fear them.

Within me there came an assurance that I had nothing to fear. One look at Cindy and I knew that she too felt that inward tranquility that makes one truly brave.

Uncle Tim waded recklessly through the swarm of creatures toward the trail that we had followed coming this way. But when I could see his face, I knew he was not reckless. He was not moved by the courage of desperation; he was animated with an inward assurance from God. I had a feeling that Uncle Tim walked with the confidence of Moses when he had stepped into the Red Sea.

I looked toward the sky. The creatures still filled the heavens. The air vibrated with their shrieks and the beating of their wings.

"Uncle Tim," I shouted, "do you notice that there is no confusion in their ranks? The first ones have moved over us rapidly, but all the others follow swiftly and orderly. They're flying northeast."

Uncle Tim did not reply. He continued his prayer. Cindy's eyes were looking up beyond the creatures.

Enoch Snow ran past me screaming and cursing. I could see creatures hanging on his face, in his hair, and on his neck. He was running as fast as he could, and at the same time was slapping at them. When he hit one, its scream was unearthly. I don't know what the creatures were, but I know they were not a product of anything earthly.

As we approached the creek, we saw Snow in one of the deep pools that filled the channel. Ducking into the water he had freed himself of most of the creatures, but his face was horrible. Shivering in the water as with the palsy, he stood neck deep, coughing and half choking.

His face was spotted by a dozen stings, and he was swelling horribly. He rubbed his face and neck with the cold water as he cursed and twisted his body in agony. Between curses a muffled groan came from his now puffy lips.

In the shallow water lay one of Snow's men, his legs kicking. Evidently severe muscular contractions caused twitching and jerking of the whole body. His mouth flew open in spasms and we heard the most vile blasphemy that could fall from the lips of a man.

Uncle Tim stopped. "Enoch, can we help you?"

With swollen lips, nostrils distended, eyes dilated, and enraged, Snow blamed us and cursed God for his sufferings. He swore that he would kill us yet. We could do no more, so we left.

We had walked no more than an hour when it became obvious that the creatures would soon be gone. Swiftly they flew northeast as if mindful of a rendezvous. Uncle Tim said:

"Steve, we've walked all night, and we haven't eaten in hours. I'm sure we don't feel like it; but open these emergency rations, and let's eat as we walk. I'm eager for us to get home. I feel sure that we are near the end of the Tribulation. I believe that by the help of God we've made it through the years of the Beast. Let's head for your old home, not the mine. If the seven years of the Beast are over, we are safe. If not, we will be as safe at home as we would be at the mine."

We walked, ate, and were silent—lost in memories. Memories of years of working, hiding, running, and of friends dying. Could it be almost over? Three people, hollow-eyed, haggard, and weary we struggled through the forest. I began to feel drowsy, but it was when I saw Cindy stagger that I knew we had to rest.

"Uncle Tim, we must rest. We've walked all night and now it is past noon."

"You're right, Steve. I was just too eager to get the news. It's my feeling that these creatures are the locusts of the ninth chapter of the Revelation. If this is true, war is on in the Holy Land and Christ will return soon."

Cindy said, "Please, Steve, I don't want to stop long. If we're going home, we can get rid of our camping equipment. That will make travel lighter. Why don't we stop just long enough to eat and be on our way?"

We agreed that Cindy's idea was best, so prepared hot food, ate freely, and drank hot coffee. During the stop, Uncle Tim, who had got drenched in the sinkhole, changed into dry clothing.

Tired but excited, we were soon on our way again. We were feeling the strain, and our muscles sent out their protests, but excitement kept us going.

It would take about a six-hour hike to get home, and it was now 2:00 in the afternoon. The wind was blowing from the north and the snow was still falling. The first two hours were the easiest. The food, short rest, and the anticipation of the news from Jerusalem kept us excited. With determination, we tramped the miles of snowy trail toward home.

However, as darkness came on, the snow became thicker. What a world! I thought. The land itself was a desolation, broken and cold. The earth had been attacked by a giant quake and an exploding sun. Men had suffered from a plague, and now they were tormented by creatures from some other world.

A full moon rose high over the world of broken trees, lighting the snow-covered land until it lay before us white and open. It was a white night filled with stars. For us it

206

was charged with expectancy. In this white darkness we walked. There were no other sounds. And within me was the pulsing thrill that we had made it through the seven years of the Beast. Our movements tonight were completely visible but this time we had no fear. It was as if the world were ours.

I came out of my dream world when I heard Cindy's teeth chattering. "Cindy, how are you making it?"

"Oh, great, Steve. I'm making it fine."

But I said, "Uncle Tim, don't you think we should take another break?"

"Yes, Steve," he answered, "we still have about two or three hours to go. I'm sure that food and some rest would help."

For a time, a bright fire cheated the cold of its victims. We felt warm, comfortable, and sleepy. But I was afraid.

"Uncle Tim, aren't we taking a chance with a fire that can be seen so easily?"

"I don't think so, Steve. If I'm right, the creatures have all the Beast's men in this area hiding or too sick to cause any trouble. Furthermore, if war has started in Jerusalem, no one will be interested in us. Snow and his men will hide from now on."

After the hot meal and more coffee, once again we were on our way, a party of three determined Christians.


But suddenly it seemed the fatigue of seven years hit me. I was just too tired to get excited about winged creatures or Jerusalem. My muscles were stiff, and exhaustion began to play tricks with my mind. Fears with which I had lived for years would not give up. What if McKifer came? Where were his dogs? Could this be a trick? Where is June? Will Matt come back? I stumbled on a rock. The fall brought me back to the present. I had actually dozed as I walked.

"Say, why don't we sing?" I asked.

"Good idea," Uncle Tim and Cindy answered in chorus.

"What do you have in mind?" Cindy's voice was surprisingly cheerful.

"It will soon be Christmas. Why don't we sing Christmas songs?" It was agreed. Our spirits lifted, and an hour later we were in sight of home.

For the first time in seven years I walked through the door feeling that I was at home to stay. But I received a stern reminder of what we had been through when I looked at Uncle Tim. His face was red with the cold. He was unshaven and thin from loss of weight. With dark rings under his eyes, he was a picture of a weary and worn man, with the exception of his eyes. They were excited. Already he was headed for the television set.

I was getting a fire started; Cindy was opening cans of emergency rations and getting a pot of coffee ready. It was a little after 10:00, and the news was already on. Someone was giving a report from Jerusalem. He had identified himself as being with the Allied Armies.

"There are reports that the Alliance of the World's army is in total disarray because of an attack by locust-like creatures with stings like scorpions. They are all over the camp. Swarms of the creatures fly over until they darken the sun. By the millions they have attacked the army. The sting is poisonous but not deadly. A Mr. Joseph Levi of our party was attacked. We have a report telling what happened and how he felt." (Later it was learned that the man was a spy for the Alliance of the World.)

Mr. Levi reported, "I felt a painful sting on my neck. It was as if someone had stuck me with a hot knife point, sending arrows of fire through my body. Almost immediately there was a twitching of the muscles in that area. This was followed by a swelling that was frightening. The pain seemed to settle in my stomach, nauseating me.

"Then the strangest thing of all happened. While I was distracted by the first sting, those creatures began a systematic coordinated attack with no preliminary circling or warning. They just came—into my hair, down my shirt collar, up my pants legs. These creatures have some kind of intelligence."

At this point the reporter picked up the story.

"I saw the victim. His face was horribly swollen and covered with red spots that were showing signs of infection. The itching was so bad that Mr. Levi said it was almost impossible not to scratch, but if the places are rubbed the infection spreads.

"Mr. Levi was in such excruciating pain that he vomited until his head dropped limply and his body writhed in convulsions. It seemed his joints would be pulled apart.

"The strangest characteristic of the creatures is their discipline. There has not been one report of an indiscriminate attack.

"To see them come is horrible. To examine one closely is an even greater shock. When one turned its head toward me and I looked at those eyes I knew that the creature was intelligent.

"They sat by the thousands on trees and bushes but they never ate so much as a leaf. An area may be filled with them, but they never attack a person who is not in the employ of the Alliance of the World.

"I have seen them cover a house like bees cover a hive. They seek an entrance at any opening. From houses where they gain entrance come the agonizing screams of stricken persons. Then the door bursts open for someone covered by the creatures to race out fighting, clawing, and cursing.

"Such happenings are isolated here in Jerusalem, but in Egypt the armies of the Alliance of the World are in confusion because of them. All the camps have been attacked.

"Israel and her allies would have been defeated in battle with the Alliance of the World if the creatures had not come when they did. And those creatures are still coming. Whatever they are, wherever they came from, they have bought time for the Allies. At this time, Israel and the Allies are saved. This is your International News Broadcast from Jerusalem."

"Well, folks, we're at the end." Uncle Tim spoke with absolute confidence. "I think we can sleep tonight in a good bed with no fear of Snow or any of his kind."

I felt exhausted. Seven years running had left its marks on all of us. When I got up from my chair, my muscles responded reluctantly. I was too utterly worn out to think further of the past or the future. I went into my old room and threw myself across the bed like a dead man. I could sleep in peace knowing the future held no terror for us.

# 12

## The King Has Come

*I heard as it were the voice of a great multitude,
and as the voice of many waters, and as the voice of
mighty thunderings, saying, Alleluia: for the Lord
God omnipotent reigneth* (Rev. 19:6).

For days we rested, soaked in hot baths, ate, listened
to the news, and slept again. These were some of the com-
forts we dreamed of most when we were people of the
night. What a joy to belong to the day again.

The news from Jerusalem made it obvious that the
end was upon us. The Allies were continuing to rush troops
and equipment into Israel. Prince Goldbar was no longer in
complete control of the world.

At the same time, most of the nations were backing
Goldbar by sending troops to Egypt. It was obvious that
Armageddon was upon us.

Cindy's spirit of planning special events came alive at
breakfast and pulled us away from the study of war.

"Uncle Tim, I want you to get a Christmas tree;
and you, Steve, try to find some Christmas decorations.
Oh, yes, and I'll need a chicken. See if you can find one
around the barn."

Enoch Snow's living at the home place had turned out to be in our favor. Had he not been here, everything would have been stolen.

"Any special kind of tree, Cindy?" Uncle Tim asked.

"Yes, the biggest you can find. This will be the best Christmas we've ever had. You find the tree, and I'll make some popcorn decorations."

Cindy was singing in the kitchen; Uncle Tim and I were whistling Christmas tunes as we went to complete our tasks. How wonderful to be free again! What a joy to walk the grounds of my youth, but how sad that all of the others were dead or lost from us. But, I reminded myself, only for a time.

As I walked toward the barn to look for a chicken and some popcorn, Cindy and her song filled my mind. It was then I really knew that all of my adult life I had yearned for someone like her, someone attractive, intelligent, and brave. How beautiful she had looked standing by the stove, her face clean and radiant, her eyes so alive and happy. What a person! How fortunate that I knew her.

Uncle Tim came in with the tree. I had caught a chicken and found some popcorn. Cindy had gathered the other things needed for Christmas. We were a happy family.

"Tomorrow is the day before Christmas. You men can trim the tree. I'll complete the cooking. I know that no one else is coming, but I'm cooking enough for a big family."

"We have plenty," I said to Cindy, "help yourself. The three and a half years of preparation that Matt, June, and I made is paying off again. Don't you wish we could have all of our family for Christmas dinner?"

Uncle Tim said, "I believe I'll listen to the late news before retiring."

"Good idea, Uncle Tim. I think I'll watch with you." He and I watched the news almost every hour of the day.

212

The whole world knew that a major battle was in the making. The news was in progress when we tuned in.

"I am speaking to you from the inside of a rock mountain called Petra. Two hours ago both sides turned loose with all the fury of modern military technology. This war is computerized and is being conducted without human compassion. There will be unprecedented destruction and unrelenting brutality. This must be what the preachers of the past called 'the end of the world.'

"To the awed inhabitants of Petra, this December 23rd will be unforgettable. Gigantic explosions cast fireballs into the sky; they open up like fiery umbrellas. Petra's ordeal by fire and explosion has begun. This may be the world's last battle.

"Let me tell you something of Petra as I have seen it. If the world lasts, generations will hear of it. Petra is about 50 miles south of the Dead Sea between the Sea and the Gulf of Aqaba. Petra was located in Jordan before Israel occupied the territory.

"Our fortress is in the remains of an ancient city with a thousand caves cut into solid rock. The whole area is located in a maze of cliffs, chasms, and awesome mountains. There is something sinister about this city. It's a place of the dead, and men have come here to die again.

"The garrison here is made up of Western allies and about 144,000 Israeli troops. We may have a total of 200,000 soldiers.

"When the Israelis took Petra from Jordan, they razed the old city to make a fort. Gun emplacements have been located in every conceivable spot, and they are protected by 30-foot reinforced concrete casements. In conventional war this is all but an impregnable fortress.

"Before the days of the Romans, Petra was developed by the Nabataeans. To get into the city one must follow the bed of a dried up stream. As you walk the twisting path, only 6 to 8 feet wide, you can never see very far ahead. The sun is shut out by overhanging rocks. On each side precipitous cliffs rise as much as 4,000 feet. After following the path for a mile, you come unexpectedly into Petra."

Suddenly, over the voice of the announcer, we heard a bell ring and a metallic voice saying, "Air raid warning red. Air raid warning red." This was followed by an ominous silence. Shortly our local station came on the air.

"We have lost contact with Petra. It is reported from Washington that the Allied Armies are in extreme danger.

"There is national news of major importance to Americans. The police of the Alliance of the World are being arrested in the United States and other Allied Nations. Prince Goldbar is threatening to retaliate. All citizens are advised to take cover immediately if an alert is sounded.

"If we are able to make contact with Petra or Jerusalem, we will do so. Until then we will continue with Christmas music."

"That's interesting," Uncle Tim said. "Since the Rapture there has been no Christmas music. Goldbar made it illegal. Things surely have changed, and they have done so in a hurry."

"But you know, Uncle Tim, the Bible prophesied that at the end of Armageddon the Beast would be defeated and he would be without allies when Christ returns. Daniel 11:45 reads, 'Yet he shall come to his end and none shall help him.'"

"I think I'll leave all this in God's hands and go to bed for a good long sleep." Uncle Tim spoke with confidence that came from a strong faith. Here we were on the edge of Armageddon, and he was able to retire. We could be bombed, but he could sleep.

The next morning, December 24, the house looked like

214

Christmas. The tree that Uncle Tim had cut filled one corner of the room. From some place all of us had brought in Christmas presents. But there was a mutual understanding that none were to be opened until after Christmas dinner the next day. We were prepared for a big Christmas. It was to be bigger than we expected.

I finally climbed wearily into bed, but with the lights out the silence became my enemy. The lonely darkness forced me to think. How will it all end? What if our army in Jerusalem is defeated? Will Goldbar turn his atomic bombs on us? Maybe we are not as safe as we think. At some late hour I gave up and slept restlessly.

Dawn came clear and cold. It took only a few minutes to have a roaring fire that extended its friendly warmth to the three of us.

Already Uncle Tim was looking for a news report from Jerusalem.

"This report is coming to you from Petra. As I speak, atomic bombs are exploding over the Allied Army. It is doubtful that any of our troops can survive outside of this rock. Thousands are being killed by explosions, heat waves, death rays, laser beams, and sound vibrations. We may not be able to hold out for the day. The next few hours will decide. The Alliance of the World has all the power needed to blast us into surrender.

"I am standing at the entrance of a cave cut in solid rock. From this point I see only a limited world, but what I see is a black and desolate world.

"If we could see the city streets and battlefields, we would see the bodies of thousands who have been killed instantly. We would see others writhing in pain, screaming in agony, and pleading for help that will never come.

"In the rock fortress we are protected, but for what? We are surrounded by a ring of fire from the army of Prince Goldbar. This may be our last broadcast.

"There is no life to be seen outside of these stone caves. Even the grass is burned away. Searing winds have left the earth smoldering. These hot winds batter against Petra. The shriek and moan like something doomed. You can hear the roar like that of a dozen jet planes in the cave with us.

"The winds make the caves stiffling. We can smell the heat, and are bathed in sweat, but we are safe from the fire.

"In desperation we watch the sky, but there is no help there. Except for the sun, we see nothing, not even a cloud or a bird. The heavens are empty.

"The blasting of atomic bombs shakes the solid rock, raising dust that chokes us. Small rocks rain from the ceiling. Soldiers drop on the floor and pray. One officer drew his knife and cut the Economic Mark from his hand.

"All of us have a foreboding of doom. We know that we'll be dead soon. How many of the Alliance army have been killed, we do not know, but they must number in the thousands. It is to be assumed that most of our troops are dead; at least, we have no contact with them.

"All around me are gaunt, unshaven men. Gloom and despair are the prevailing spirits, although invisible men in caves throughout Petra battle furiously. If an enemy plane approaches, the guns of Petra challenge it, but we know now that it is only a show. There is no relief coming and we cannot save ourselves. There is a rumor, however, that an air fleet of 50,000 planes is on the way. I find myself wanting to believe this, but reality tells me that it is fiction.

"This is John Farmer in Petra. The crew and I are preparing to make a try for the Command Tunnel. I return you to Washington."

"Uncle Tim, Steve, breakfast is ready." Cindy's voice

and the smell of the hot food were enough to draw us from our television set.

Even as I enjoyed breakfast, I could not escape the vision that I had of Petra.

"Uncle Tim, I would like to see Petra. Conditions are such that we can't receive clear pictures of the place, but I am fascinated by it. During the Millennial Reign I think I'll visit the area. In fact, I'd like to write some documentations on the last battle."

"Why not, Steve? During the thousand years of the Millennial Reign of Christ people will still be people. Cars will be rolling, planes flying, and people busy. I think you can visit Petra if you wish."

Following breakfast Uncle Tim returned to the news, and I stayed to help Cindy with the dishes.

"Steve, I'm going to prepare one of the biggest and best dinners that I've ever cooked. Tomorrow will be a Christmas to remember."

I did not have time to respond.

"Steve, quick!" Uncle Tim called. "Farmer is continuing his report from the Command Tunnel."

"We are standing in the entrance of the Command Tunnel. From here I can show you the Valley of Petra. You will observe that all combustible materials have been burned away. The walls of the cliffs have been seared black by the bomb blasts.

"There is no way an army can survive such destruction. Although we are in a place perfectly designed by nature for defense, the shelling has been savage. We have been surrounded by devastating explosions. The heat following an atomic blast is almost intolerable even when one is deep in a cave of solid rock.

"The enemy has incalculable firepower and is blasting us with a continuous barrage. At times, the whole area seems to be on fire. Thick clouds of dust and fire swirl

217

in the air as the mountains shake. Without air or land support, Petra cannot be supplied and will collapse.

"The commanding officer has just announced that he has no alternative to surrender. An awesome silence has fallen over the command room. No one moves or makes a sound.

"The silence has just been broken by a young Jewish officer who brought an announcement. Tears are running down his cheeks. Suddenly most of the men are crying like babies.

"Here is the official communique, just handed to me. 'This is the commander of the Allied armies. Petra will be surrendered to the Alliance of the World at 12:00 noon tomorrow, 25 December. Food and water supplies will not last another 24 hours. History will record that no army ever fought better than this one. No men were ever braver than these. No soldiers endured more. And no troops ever fought more gallantly. But spirit, courage, and determination cannot defeat laser beams, shock guns, and atomic bombs. May God protect the world.'"

We turned from the television set, as gloom settled over us. Somehow we had expected a miracle of deliverance. We tried to stay busy to keep our minds off the defeated men of Petra.

It was near midnight, Christmas Eve, before we had the courage to listen to the news that could be Petra's last report.

The picture came on with a closeup of an Allied soldier. His eyes were wild, his arms waving like a windmill. He was hysterically shouting, "No surrender! No surrender! The air armada is coming. Fifty thousand planes are on their way. They're coming in from the East."

"The scene is wild!" John Farmer screamed. "More men are rushing in. All are shouting the same news: The air armada is coming in from the East!'

"I can see it now. The fleet is completely filling the sky. We'll have pictures in just a moment. The heavens are aglow with a strange light all around the armada. The place is wild with excitement. A general just ran past crying, 'We're saved! We're saved!'"

I did not listen any further. I was struggling with the door trying to get out of our house. How well I remembered the bright moonlight seven years ago. Could this be . . . ? It must be! I would soon know. I ran into the yard. It was midnight, but as light as the brightest day. Out of the East there flowed a radiant light, a soft light, an inspiring light.

The eastern sky was filled with what at that distance appeared to be large white birds. They moved in many directions to fill all the heavens. I could see neither star nor moon but only the white creatures that seemed to be approaching the earth.

I kept thinking, All over the world billions of people are watching the sky right now; all are seeing the snow-white creatures that fill the heavens.

My thoughts were interrupted. "Listen," Cindy spoke quietly beside me. "Listen."

It was only when she spoke that I realized Cindy and Uncle Tim had followed me into the yard. As I reached for Cindy's hand I shouted joyously, "We've made it, Cindy! We've made it!"

The long bank of whiteness spread rapidly from the East. When it was nearer, it seemed to fill the heavens with a sea of distinct bodies. No night could have been brighter, yet there was no moon.

We waited and watched. Then I understood why Cindy had said, "Listen." First, it was a faint sound then clearer and louder. Voices! Voices singing!

Those white beings were people clothed in radiant garments. They were led by a mighty angel. The multitude spoke with a voice that filled the earth. "Let us be glad and rejoice, and give honor to him: for the marriage of the Lamb is come, and His wife hath made herself ready. And to her was granted that she should be arrayed in fine linen, clean and white: for the fine linen is the righteousness of saints" (Rev. 19:7-8).

We stood in hypnotic fascination at the sight and sound. We watched the sky filled with "a great multitude, which no man could number, of all nations, and kindreds, and people, and tongues . . . clothed with white robes, and palms in their hands; and cried with a loud voice, saying, Salvation to our God which sitteth upon the throne. . . . Blessing, and glory, and . . . honour, and power, and might be unto our God for ever and ever."[1]

"Cindy," Uncle Tim's voice brought us back to earth and to immediate reality, "I'm glad you cooked such a large Christmas dinner. There'll be quite a crowd with all the family here! CHRIST THE KING HAS COME!"

---

1. Rev. 7:9-12.

220